'You look absolutely marvellous,' Connor said, and heard the shake in his voice. He couldn't help himself; he bent over and kissed her lightly on the cheek. He felt her shock, but when she raised her eyes to his they were pleased.

'You look pretty good yourself,' she said.

He sat opposite, puzzling over the slight anxiety he could hear in her voice. 'Are you nervous?' he asked in disbelief. 'Let's make a pact—tonight, neither of us is to think of anything except the present. Time out, as it were. After all, Cinderella wasn't worried that at midnight the coach and horses would turn back into a pumpkin and rats. She went ahead and enjoyed herself anyway.' Connor leaned forward and clinked his glass against hers. 'To a wonderful evening to come.'

'One night of magic?' She then bit her lip and studie you've convinced me. To to come.'

Tonight
whatever

**Gill Sanderson**, aka Roger Sanderson, started writing as a husband-and-wife team. At first Gill created the storyline, characters and background, asking Roger to help with the actual writing. But her job became more and more time-consuming, and he took over all of the work. He loves it!

Roger has written many Medical™ Romance books for Harlequin Mills & Boon. Ideas come from three of his children—Helen is a midwife, Adam a health visitor, Mark a consultant oncologist. Weekdays are for work; weekends find Roger walking in the Lake District or Wales.

**Recent titles by the same author:**

CHRISTMAS AT RIVERCUT MANOR
THE COUNTRY DOCTOR'S DAUGHTER
THE MIDWIFE AND THE SINGLE DAD
A MOTHER FOR HIS SON

# VILLAGE MIDWIFE, BLUSHING BRIDE

BY
## GILL SANDERSON

MILLS & BOON

First published in Great Britain 2010
Harlequin Mills & Boon Limited,
Eton House, 18-24 Paradise Road, Richmond, Surrey TW9 1SR

© Gill Sanderson 2010

ISBN: 978 0 263 87917 9

Harlequin Mills & Boon policy is to use papers that are natural, renewable and recyclable products and made from wood grown in sustainable forests. The logging and manufacturing process conform to the legal environmental regulations of the country of origin.

Printed and bound in Spain
by Litografia Rosés, S.A., Barcelona

# VILLAGE MIDWIFE, BLUSHING BRIDE

*For Emma and Adam, the bravest couple I know*

# PROLOGUE

DR CONNOR MAITLAND lay on the examination couch. He was pretty sure he knew what the verdict would be. He just needed to hear the neurologist—his friend, Mick Baxter—confirm it. 'Well?'

Mick gave a regretful sigh. 'I'm afraid you're right, Connor. It looks as though you are well and truly on the mend.'

Relief coursed through Connor, swift and invigorating. 'Excellent. It'll be nice to have my life back. Although I am, of course, sorry to curtail your source of future research.'

Mick grinned. 'I should think so too. What sort of friend contracts the worst case of Lyme disease I've ever come across—the neurological complications were phenomenal—and then makes such a rapid recovery?'

'You call twelve months rapid?'

'Compared to what I was originally expecting, yes. Still, I should get a nice paper out of you for the next symposium.'

Connor frowned as his friend continued to check him over. There had been times this last year when he'd wondered why he was striving to get better, but it had never occurred to him that he might not make it eventually. 'I was that bad?' he said.

Mick placed cool fingers on the pulse point in his wrist. 'You were. Did I forget to mention it?'

'You know you did! You told me every gloomy possibility

in the book bar that. It beats me how someone with such an appalling bedside manner can be one of the best men in his field.'

'Lucky for you that I am. If you and Francine hadn't been having dinner with me when you—' He broke off, frowning slightly.

'Yes, yes,' said Connor impatiently. 'Only Dr Mick Baxter would have spotted that my bout of flu, following a climbing weekend in the Lake District where I picked up a rogue tick the size of a pinhead, was actually undiagnosed Lyme disease. I'm not ungrateful, Mick. What I want to know is how soon I can start work again.'

Mick made a note, his face troubled. 'I said you were on the mend, not fully recovered. You went untreated for a significant period, which means problems with the nervous system are more likely to recur than if you'd been caught early. We've discussed this. You're never going to be the top-flight surgeon you were a year ago. I can understand your frustration, but you need to take it easy to begin with. Assist, perhaps. Or teach.'

'I hate teaching and I refuse to be a second-string anything. I know exactly what I want to do. All those months lying on my back staring out of hospital windows gave me plenty of time to think. I'm going to pick up my GP training again. I'm going to be the best damn GP in the country.'

'Now *that's* an interesting idea,' said Mick, sounding thoughtful as he scribbled another note. 'I'd forgotten you started off in that direction before deciding to specialise in surgery. But it's stressful, mate.'

Connor smiled. 'I've held a man's heart in my hand, knowing if my scalpel slipped a quarter of an inch he'd be dead. That's stress.'

'Which you never used to feel. You were the coolest man in Theatre I've ever seen and that was great. Things are different now.'

Mick's hand moved to assess the blood flow in the throat artery. After a year of such examinations, Connor hardly noticed any more. He had thought it all out. After finishing GP training he would buy into a practice in the countryside. Somewhere he could climb and walk whenever he felt hemmed in. Somewhere with a day surgery unit, perhaps, so he could still put his skills to good use. And a big enough practice where there would always be other doctors to cover his duties if he had a relapse. Which Mick had told him months ago would remain a possibility.

'Do you ever hear from Francine, by the way?' said Mick.

Despite the warmth of the day, Connor felt suddenly chilly. 'No.'

'Oh, I thought she might have kept in touch. She does with quite a lot of the crowd.'

'Not with me.'

'Pity. You used to be a golden couple.'

'We were a golden couple when I was a top rank surgeon and she was being head-hunted by medical institutions all down the West Coast of America. My transfer to the long-term sick list rather took the shine off our relationship.'

'Go on,' murmured Mick.

'I don't need to. You know it all. She couldn't face the thought that I might be permanently ill. We'd split up even before she shook the UK dust off her boots and took the job in San Francisco. Mick, you were the one who sat up all night with me preventing me from drowning my sorrows with illicit booze and doing my disaster area of a nervous system even more damage. Why are you dragging it up again now?'

'Because when I so much as mention her name your pulse speeds up, your breathing gets faster and I'll bet your blood pressure is up too.'

'That's normal, isn't it? We were together for two years. I'd have to be made of concrete not to feel anything at all.'

Mick was silent for a moment. Connor could sense him working out exactly what he needed to say. 'Listen, Connor. For you as a surgeon, the patient is a body—the mind plays very little part in what you do to it. I'm a neurologist. My patients are mostly awake. And I'm conscious of just how much the mind and the body interact.'

'So?' Connor was aware that his voice sounded harsh.

'You're over the initial shock of contracting the illness at all. You're making astounding progress physically. You've accepted the need for a change in career—and for the record, by the way, I think you'll be a terrific GP—but the thought of Francine still stresses you.'

That again. Mick was like a terrier with a rat. Connor could admire him as a colleague even while he wished he'd give up where he himself was concerned. 'Stop right there. Francine herself doesn't upset me. I have no feelings for *her* at all. It's what she did that still rankles.'

'You mean leaving you when you were a helpless invalid?' Mick leaned back, considering him. 'I get the feeling there's more to it, Connor. And you'll never be as good a doctor as you can be until you've come to terms with whatever that was.'

Connor gave a short laugh. 'It'll pass. And don't worry— I'll take care not to get into the same situation again.'

'If you say so.' Mick's phone rang and he frowned as he picked up the receiver. 'My secretary knows I'm busy with you; she usually doesn't interrupt for—Pardon?…About time too. I'll come and get them.' He replaced the phone. 'Start getting dressed, Connor. I'll be right back.'

Connor wondered what was important enough to interrupt a consultation. Something serious, evidently. It was fifteen minutes before Mick returned and when he did his face was troubled.

'Bad news?' said Connor.

'I'm afraid so. I've just phoned the path lab, asked if there was any chance they'd made a mistake, but they said no. I did warn you about this, mate. I told you it was a remote possibility, but you've made such a good recovery that I hoped…'

Connor was getting a nasty feeling about whatever was coming. 'Mick! Just tell me. Don't wrap it up; just tell me!'

Mick took a deep breath. 'I've just had the report on the last set of samples I sent along to the lab. Everything's in remission, all your stats are fine except…'

'Except?'

'There's no easy way to say this. Connor, you're infertile. The chances of you fathering children from now on are negligible.'

Connor stared at Mick, unable to speak. He felt as if he'd just been dropped into a wasteland. Yes, he had his life back, he would regain his strength and go on to make a new career— but for what? All his dreams for the future had included a large, boisterous family. Sons and daughters who would grow up to make him proud.

The silence between them stretched on. Eventually Mick said, 'I'm so sorry. But it's not the end of the world. There's always a chance that some future treatment will become available or…'

'Don't bother, Mick. I'm a doctor; I know the statistics. I've just got to live with it.' He couldn't avoid the bitter addition. 'Somehow.'

'I know you will. Anyone less strong wouldn't have made the progress that you already have.' But Mick's eyes were still concerned. 'I wish I could do more, Connor, but I can't. You know I'm off to Patagonia next week to start this new neurological unit? It could be years before I come back. I've handed your case over to Dr Evan Price. He's a first-rate man. He'll want to see you every six months or so, and you can call on him any time.'

'You introduced us at my last appointment.' An older,

distant man, Connor remembered. He had an excellent reputation—but he'd never be a friend. Well, he didn't need
friends. Not now.

Connor walked out of the hospital grounds not feeling the
warmth of the sun on his back. Around him were hurrying
visitors, importantly-striding medical staff. You could tell
the difference between them and the patients who'd come
out of the building for fresh air, for a change from the san-
itised life of the wards. The patients moved slowly—as he
had done himself until he'd made the conscious decision
to reclaim his life. He was a doctor—he refused to be a
patient any more.

He thought about what Mick had said before the path lab
report had arrived. Essentially that he had to let go of the past
in order to move forward. Easier said than done, especially
now. Connor had a vivid memory of the weekend before everything started to fall apart. He and Francine had spent it
climbing. They'd tested each other on the challenging
stretches, laughed and made plans for the future. But some
time during those forty-eight hours he'd contracted Lyme
disease, and his life had changed for ever.

He'd told the truth when he said Francine was no longer
anything to him emotionally. The rational part of him didn't
blame her for taking her splendid new job and heading for new
and more magnificent slopes. There had been no guarantee
back then that he would ever get better.

Her legacy, however, was something else. The irrational
part of him was still immeasurably hurt by the emptiness of
her previous declarations of undying love. That was what had
tormented his mind during those terrible days when he
couldn't even move his body. He'd vowed then that it would
never happen again. He would never again let anyone get
close enough to betray him. And, once he'd decided that, he'd

locked all the feelings away. Including the shock of her last careless, unthinking act.

Now, the consequences of that act, combined with this final stroke of the whip, threatened to unlock all those feelings again. Connor set his jaw. He wouldn't let it happen. Stone. That was what he would be—stone.

# CHAPTER ONE

ENOUGH, decided Zoe.

The boxes holding their immediate necessities had been unpacked. Jamie's bedroom looked as much as possible like the one they had said goodbye to this morning because she thought he needed that reassurance. Now he wanted to play in the garden and the adrenalin that had been carrying Zoe through the day had just run out. She took a mug of tea to the patio and sat on the wooden bench, breathing in the heavy scent of honeysuckle and turning her face to the early evening sun.

*Please let this be the right decision.*

Tomorrow she would be back to work as a midwife but this was a new world, as different as it could be from their London flat with the busy streets outside. She wondered if she would fit in.

Here the sky was clear, trees stirred gently above the shrubs, and in the distance she could see the tip of a green hill with the faint tracery of grey limestone walls across it. And it was quiet! Just Jamie murmuring to himself as he pottered about and the chirping of birds settling down for the night. For a moment Zoe felt very alone.

Their new home was a converted coach house, small but perfect for the two of them. Zoe hoped it was a place where she could settle, could come to terms with the past, where

Jamie could grow up, where the pain they had both suffered would be absorbed by the building of a new life.

Not quite new. The coach house had only been part-furnished: if Zoe turned her head she could see her own sofa in the living room. The furniture she had brought with her dovetailed with what was already here, the new and the old combined. That was as it should be—you shouldn't ever entirely forget the past. But she would learn to live with it, learn to distance herself from Neil's progression from happy-go-lucky registrar to an alcoholic who prioritised his addiction over his family. She and Jamie would be happy again.

'Mummy, can I ride my bike now? Please?'

Where did he get his energy? Zoe looked down at her son and smiled, her heart turning over. 'Just up and down the path, sweetheart. It's getting late and I'm too tired to find you a longer ride today.'

'Can't I ride over there?'

*Over there* was the lane outside. She could see why he'd be confused. It didn't seem like any road he'd been taught to be careful of and he was used to riding in the park near their flat where there were long paths looking very similar.

'No, that's a road. We drove up it. You're not to go out of the garden ever unless I'm with you.'

Zoe hadn't had a garden for years. Jamie had never had one. They'd be able to plant things here; not just what would fit in a window box, but a whole bush or a big swathe of bulbs. Something else that was new. This garden was safe and enclosed—Jamie could roam it at will without her worrying. It would be like having a miniature park of his own.

'Can I go through the other gate? There's a longer bit of path there and there's a slope.' As an extra argument, Jamie added, 'I promise to be careful.'

Other gate? Zoe roused herself to look where her son was pointing. The path ran from their kitchen door, down the garden and into the garden of the big house next door. Then it disappeared into a stand of small trees. Where the post-and-rail fence crossed the path was a rustic-looking gate.

'No, sweetheart. That's Dr Maitland's garden. He's our landlord. We have to stay on our side.'

'All right,' said Jamie. 'I'll go for just a little ride then.'

Zoe watched, grateful that he was adapting. She didn't know how much he remembered of that dreadful day. He'd had terrible dreams to start with and for weeks he had hardly spoken. Even now, occasionally she found him hiding behind the furniture, completely silent. She had told him Daddy was in Heaven, still loving him, but she wasn't sure how much he'd taken in. She hoped the move from city to country would help turn him back into the joyous little boy he had been before the accident.

Certainly he seemed content at the moment, riding his bike up and down the path, and Zoe was thankful. In a new house—and starting a new school tomorrow—he needed all the confidence he could get.

Zoe wasn't surprised when Jamie chose *The Big Red Tractor* for his bedtime story. It was comfort-reading and the fact that they both knew it by heart made no difference to his love of it.

He was asleep by the end, and Zoe was hardly less tired. It had been a long day, supervising the removal men then driving up all the way from London. There was more unpacking to do yet, but instead she sat holding her son's hand as the sun sank.

Her mobile rang in the bedroom next door. Zoe ran to answer before it woke Jamie.

'Are you settled? Have you eaten? Did you find the casserole? Are you *sure* you don't want me to come and help?'

Zoe curled up on the bed, smiling. Dear, lovely Jo Summers, her best friend since the day they'd started midwifery training together. Despite living a hundred miles away, Jo had been the first person to arrive at Zoe's side on that horrific evening when a drunken Neil had crashed his car, killing himself and only by a miracle not taking Jamie with him. Jo had steered Zoe through the formalities, shielded her from the nightmares, and supported her throughout the funeral.

'Hi, Jo. I'm fine,' said Zoe. 'The casserole was gorgeous. But I'm exhausted, I'm going to bed and I'll see you at work first thing in the morning.'

Her friend was the reason she and Jamie were here. Jo was now her husband's practice manager in the Derbyshire market town of Buckley and when the community midwife position fell vacant she had been in no doubt as to who should fill it. Zoe remembered the energy that had tumbled out of the letter…

*…know you are coping, you always do, but you can't tell me you're happy. You need a complete change and so does Jamie—probably more than you. Forget the hospital, love. You've liked Buckley when you've come on visits—now come for real and be our practice midwife. The primary school is just next door to the surgery and, what's more, I can find you a ready-made home that I know you'll love. It's a converted coach house at the bottom of the garden belonging to one of our doctors. Please say yes, Zoe. Sam and I won't tell anybody what Neil was really like. It'll be a chance for a fresh start for you and Jamie.*

Zoe shook herself back to the present. Jo was still talking. '…really sorry we couldn't get out of Sam's auntie's eightieth to help you move in, but there you go. Have you met Connor yet?'

That would be her new landlord. 'No.'

'Oh, I thought he might have popped over. He must have been out on one of his hikes. Anyway, don't worry. Once you get to know him, he'll be fine.'

Zoe hadn't been worried—until now. A faint anxiety stirred. 'What do you mean, once I get to know him?'

'Nothing. I'm blethering. I'm just so pleased you're finally here.'

'Me too. Thanks for everything, Jo.' Zoe clicked the phone off.

A late bee buzzed against the honeysuckle. Zoe shooed it away and closed the window. From upstairs it was possible to see part of Dr Connor Maitland's house. Lights flashed on; he must have just come home.

It was a big house for one man. Zoe had hoped her landlord would have children for Jamie to play with, but apparently he lived by himself. 'He's got a brother and two sisters,' Jo had said, 'but he doesn't see much of them.'

Zoe had felt a twinge of envy. She would have loved to be part of a big family. 'They don't visit often?'

'Not as often as he needs. And he never goes up to see them. I've always liked the look of the house, though, so when it came on the market I told him places like that were in short supply and it was a bargain.'

'Jo!' If her friend had one fault, it was a tendency to manage other people's lives.

'What? Running this practice isn't just a question of medicine. Three years Connor's been here now. That's too long to live a hermit existence. Room for his relations was vital. They'd be good for him.'

A hermit existence, indeed. The poor man probably just couldn't cope with Jo's particular brand of bonhomie. As Zoe gazed at the house she saw a dark figure come out of French windows at the back. Dr Maitland himself, she presumed. He sat on a seat and sipped from the mug in his hand. She knew it was now too dark for him to see her but she still moved back a little.

Because the figure was just an outline, it looked odd—menacing or lonely, she didn't know which. Normally, she would have made herself presentable and walked across to introduce herself. But she was tired, and Jamie might wake and panic, and…and the figure seemed to want to be alone. Zoe was very familiar with that time at the end of the day when all you wanted was to be able to sit—and not think. Dr Maitland would be at the surgery tomorrow. She'd say hello then.

Connor was tidying up the small theatre suite. Nobody worried about rank at Buckley Medical Centre. The place needed to be left ready in case of emergency but they were short-handed today. He'd finished his list for the morning so he was the one getting clean scrubs out of the dryer and putting them ready on the shelves. Truth to tell, he liked doing it. Post-surgery was always an awkward time for him—this gave him a chance to wind down.

He shook out the last few items from the tumble dryer with rather more force than was necessary, thinking of the life he'd lost. He was making a go of it as a GP, but it was sometimes difficult to feel the sense of fulfilment he'd hoped for—especially on a surgery day. Suturing injuries and doing joint injections assisted by one chatty scrub-cum-practice nurse was a far cry from the lifesaving operations he'd used to excel at. He closed his eyes for a moment, remembering the team of top-notch personnel in the theatre, the bright clear lights, the tension. It was…hard coming down to this. His grandma had always said pride went before a fall. Connor now knew what she meant. He hoped his courteous manner towards the patients never changed, but he was aware that his ambivalent feelings often made him short with his colleagues in the practice. Having this time alone after surgery helped him to adjust all over again to the way his life had changed.

Zoe's head was whirling at the speed with which Jo had propelled her on an induction tour of the medical centre. Originally it had been a large Victorian house built, presumably, for a large Victorian family, but it had been added to and modernised over the years. Now there were rooms everywhere. There were even two four-bed wards left over from its cottage hospital days. These were used for overnight stays or emergencies when Buckley was cut off by snow or floods.

'And this is the day-surgery suite,' said Jo, turning into yet another corridor. 'If we're short-handed and you're not busy, I might ask you to assist sometimes. You've still got up-to-date scrub-nurse certificates, haven't you?'

'Oh, yes—it pays to be multi-talented.' It had been an easy skill to acquire—and, the way Neil had run through money at times, Zoe had been glad of the security that occasional extra shift-work had brought.

Jo had just opened the door when her mobile handset went. 'Sorry, my next visitor's arrived early. Oh, good, you're still here, Connor. This is Zoe Hilton, our new midwife and your new tenant. I've got to fly. Walk her back to my office when you've introduced yourselves, would you? There's a love.' And, with a gentle push on Zoe's back, Jo was gone.

Zoe found herself propelled into a small laundry room. As with everything else at Buckley, it was hospital-style in miniature. Enough like her normal working environment to be comforting, unlike enough to be disconcerting.

'Exit one practice manager who only ever moves at full speed,' the occupant of the room said drily. 'It makes working here stimulating.'

Zoe turned around—and gaped. He was fabulous! Why hadn't Jo warned her? Probably she'd thought she was past being influenced by a man's looks. After all, Neil had been fantastically good-looking, and see where that had got her—to devastating, long drawn out heartbreak. She'd vowed *never again* and she'd meant it, but still, this man took her breath away!

'Jo's always been that way,' she said, trying to beat down the shocking feeling of attraction. 'I've known her for years.'

Connor Maitland was nothing like Neil, but somehow he was even more striking. He was wearing shapeless green scrubs that nevertheless indicated a muscular body beneath them. He was tall, wiry, with dark hair a bit longer than was fashionable. Deep lines on his face suggested there had been a period of considerable pain in his life, but otherwise that face was... Oh, for goodness' sake, Zoe! What was she doing, standing like a dumbstruck schoolgirl? Get a grip!

She walked over, reached for his proffered hand and... 'Ow!' She rubbed her palm vigorously. 'Did you see that? There was a spark. It jumped from your hand to mine. And it hurt.'

Dr Maitland seemed equally shaken. He snapped his eyes away from hers and cleared his throat. 'Static electricity. It's a dry day and I've just been emptying the dryer. I must have been charged and you earthed me.'

Charged? Earthed? Zoe knew about static electricity, of course; sometimes when she pulled her silk nightdress over her head she could see the tiny sparks flashing from her body. But never had she felt a spark jump from someone's body to hers.

He put out his hand again. 'It's not a nice way to greet a new colleague, is it? Shocking her? I hope we'll get on better in the future.'

She took his hand warily. No spark this time, but *something*, nonetheless. His palm was warm and smooth. His handshake was firm and his eyes had been drawn back to her face as if he was using this act of greeting to get a line on her character. He unsettled her from top to toe—and already this had gone on too long. She let go.

He seemed equally glad to break contact. 'So,' he said briskly. 'Welcome to the practice, Zoe.' She must have looked surprised at his use of her first name because he gave a slight smile and said, 'I can tell you're from a big hospital. We don't stand on ceremony here. How has your day been so far?'

She had to say something. Lord knew what he would think of her if she were silent much longer. 'Fine,' she managed. 'Bewildering. Different. But interesting. I'm looking forward to working here. Everyone seems very friendly.'

'We try to be. Within a professional framework, obviously.'

Was that a warning? Jo had indicated that he didn't encourage relationships. Well, he would have no problems with *her* not being professional. She inclined her head stiffly.

There was an awkward silence. Dr Maitland appeared to think all the social requirements had been fulfilled. 'Would you like to see the rest of the suite?' he asked, clearly casting around for something to say. 'Not that you'll need it. The maternity unit you'll be using is at Sheffield.'

'Thank you. I'd like that.'

Zoe had spent her entire working life in large city hospitals. She believed implicitly in the centralisation of expertise. But, walking through the small scrub room and then into the cut-down version of a theatre, she felt a tugging nostalgia for the days when the cottage hospital at Buckley would have looked after its locals from the cradle to the grave. She turned to ask politely whether there were a lot of day-surgery cases. The words died on her tongue. Connor Maitland had subtly altered. In this theatre he wore his shapeless scrubs like a badge of office. A sharp shiver went through Zoe. Also a stab of interest. She knew the phenomenon well. The man had presence and this was his natural element! What on earth was he doing in a provincial medical centre?

She was too occupied with memorising doors and staircases on the way back to Jo's office to make conversation.

When Connor nodded at the nameplate and made to leave she was taken by surprise. 'Thank you,' she said, scrambling for words. 'Oh, and thank you for renting us the house. It's lovely.'

'It was your friend's idea. Thank her.' And he was gone, heading down the hallway.

Zoe stared after him. What did *that* mean? The words hadn't been unfriendly as such, just indifferent. You'd think he'd want to say *something* about the lease and the house. Nor had he acknowledged the spark when they'd shaken hands. Not the real, live flash that had glowed brightly for an instant and then disappeared, but the spark of a totally different kind that had flashed between them. She was sure she hadn't imagined Connor's telltale widening of the eyes. He was obviously a better actor than her and had his own reasons for holding back. It was odd, but it suited her fine. She didn't want complications. She'd follow his example, but *not* to the point of rudeness like him.

'Okay, give,' she said to Jo as soon as her friend was free. 'Tell me about your Dr Maitland.'

'Hmm?' said Jo unconvincingly.

'Why, for example, does he walk around your Theatre like a lion? And why does a man that sinfully attractive live on his own?'

'He's not married,' Jo said after a pause. 'Never has been, as far as I know. No girlfriend either, not since he's been with us. He's…been ill. He socialises when he has to, but he prefers to keep himself to himself.'

Zoe didn't miss Jo's dissatisfied tone. 'It's not a crime,' she said with a chuckle. But she recalled those lines of etched pain and grieved for him. *He's…been ill.* That must have been some trauma.

Ah, well, Jo would tell her when she was good and ready. In the meantime, Zoe would respect Connor's privacy. Quite apart from anything else, it would prevent her from making a fool of herself if any more 'sparks' occurred between them. She'd been so shaken. She hadn't felt a sensation like it for years. There had been that sudden wish to know him, the physical attraction that made her mouth dry and her body feel warm. She would have to guard very carefully against that. As she had already proved, she was the world's worst judge of suitable partners for a relationship. Neil had wounded her so badly, wounded her and compromised Jamie's safety—Zoe was never going to commit herself again. All she wanted was a quiet life with her son.

To Zoe's great relief, Jamie had enjoyed his first day at his new school. This morning's nerves when he'd donned the Buckley Primary sweatshirt for the first time had vanished and he was smiling more than he had for a while.

'I've done a picture for you, Mummy,' he said, waving a rolled-up piece of paper as she crossed the playground.

Zoe unrolled it straight away. 'Oh, sweetheart!' Happy tears prickled in her eyes when she saw that his usual square block of flats had been replaced by an unpractised house-shape.

'It's our new house,' Jamie said importantly, 'and that's me and that's the path where I ride my bike, and that's you and…and that's Daddy in Heaven, looking down on us.'

Zoe looked at the stick figure at the top of the piece of paper and bit her lip. She was so thankful that Jamie had never understood what his father really was. 'It's very good,' she managed to say. 'We'll stick it on the fridge with your magnets when we get home.'

It was a warm evening. Zoe changed out of her uniform with relief, putting on shorts and a thin top. Her head ached from trying to absorb all the information in her patients' records ready for her first clinic tomorrow. She undid her hair from its neat pleat and shook it down round her shoulders. That was better—loose and free.

Then she sat outside and had a long glass of lemonade. In London they'd had a balcony, five floors above the traffic. It was better than nothing, but this was the real thing. A patio with a wooden table, two wicker chairs and a bench. And it caught the evening sun! Marvellous. She thought she might spend quite a lot of time out here—once all her boxes were unpacked, that was.

Jamie was riding up and down the path, making motorbike noises. Zoe winced at the all too accurate shriek-of-brakes sound he made at the end of the path. 'What do you want for tea?' she called.

'Scones,' came the instant reply.

Zoe smiled. He really was happy, then. Scones were Jamie's all-time favourite. He liked to help mix the dough and press the lumps into their special baking tray with funny faces built into the patty tins.

Then she had a tiny revelation. He wouldn't have to make the dough with her here. He could stay outside on his bike. The gate to the lane was firmly shut, and she could keep an eye on him through the kitchen window. This really was a wonderful place.

Zoe had a small tussle with the unfamiliar cooker, but the scones were soon done, currents fixed in as eyes. She'd just split and buttered the first one when she heard wails. Jamie! Her heart pounded in sudden uncontrollable fear—what had happened? She rushed outside with the scone still in her hand and there was her crying son…in the arms of Connor Maitland!

'Mummy,' wailed Jamie, even louder than before. Zoe reached out and grabbed him, hugging him to her in relief. She rocked him backwards and forwards, murmuring words of comfort. The muffled sobs quietened.

'A minor accident,' said Connor. He looked awkward and ill at ease. 'I was just passing and he fell off the gate. I think he was curious about my garden and climbed up to peer across—

and was startled when I appeared round the corner. The bar gave way. I've had a quick look at him; there doesn't seem to be any serious damage. A bit of a shock and a grazed knee.'

'Thank you! I was looking out of the window all the time, but…'

'Children can get into trouble at a minute's notice. It's part of the growing up process.' He smiled at Jamie. 'That looks a nice scone. Is it still warm?'

Zoe looked down. In her fright over Jamie, she hadn't even registered that he'd jammed the scone in his mouth. She smiled shakily. That was why he'd gone quiet. You couldn't cry if you were eating.

Jamie considered Connor solemnly over the top of it. 'Mummy made it.' He considered a moment longer. 'Would you like a bite? It had a face on the bottom but I've eated most of it.'

'Jamie! It's not polite to…'

'Thank you very much.' To Zoe's surprise, Connor's answer came before she'd finished talking. Jamie stretched out his hand—not letting go of the scone—and Connor took a small bite. 'Very nice indeed,' he said.

Zoe was recovering. 'Would you like one of your own? I've got a whole plateful.'

He hesitated, seemed to answer out of politeness. 'Yes, please. Do they all have faces?'

Jamie nodded. 'Funny faces.'

Zoe turned to get the scones, then realised Connor was following. There was a brief moment when he seemed too big for the kitchen. With her arms full of Jamie, she nodded helplessly at the plate.

'Thank you.' He took a scone. 'I have my own now,' he said to Jamie. 'Would you like your bite back?'

Jamie thought a moment. 'That's all right,' he said generously. 'You have it all.' He wriggled to get down.

Zoe retreated to the sink, ostensibly to wash her hands. Jamie was no trouble now. But she had to deal with Connor. In her kitchen. And he was still doing fluttery things to her insides. He looked cool but smart, dressed in lightweight khaki trousers and a pristine white shirt. She guessed he'd be going back to run a surgery later. Embarrassment flooded her as she glanced down at her own clothes—or lack of them. Her shorts were…well, short. Her white T-shirt top was old, made of thin cotton; it did little to hide her generous figure. And across the bust was written the message, *Ask me: I might.* She had won it in a hospital raffle ages ago. What kind of a colleague, what kind of a neighbour would he think she was? She fought the urge to pull an apron off the door hook—it would only serve to emphasize what she was trying to conceal. He might not even have noticed.

'You're good with children,' she said into the silence. 'Is that personal experience?'

For a moment it seemed as if a dark shadow passed across his face. His answer was curt. 'In a way. Not my own, but I have several nieces and nephews. I like children. They're… honest. Not like adults. Children say what they think and mean. It's refreshing.'

'Refreshing is one way of putting it,' muttered Zoe. 'Embarrassing is another.'

'That sounded heartfelt,' he said, then looked as if he could kick himself for prolonging the conversation.

'It was. We don't see much of my family,' she explained, feeling disloyal. 'They live in Jersey and don't often leave the island. But one time they were in London for a reunion dinner and Jamie said—very loudly—of my mother, "I don't like Grandma."'

'Oh, dear. And is she likeable?'

'She's all right. She's just not used to small children.'

'She had you,' pointed out Connor.

'I was a late baby and an only child. I'm not sure they quite knew what to do with me. We were happy enough, but then Dad was killed with his regiment and Mum went to pieces. For a long time she treated me more like an adult companion than a daughter.' So much so that Zoe hadn't realised until much later that her mother had been suffocating her.

'That must have been hard.'

Zoe shrugged off his concern, even though it warmed her. 'I didn't know any different,' she said lightly. 'Anyway, she's remarried now, one of Dad's fellow officers. He was a widower.' And Mum was back to her brisk, army wife self. It was a relief in a lot of ways.

Connor had finished his scone. His eyes were flicking around the kitchen. Zoe was uneasily aware that she hadn't unpacked everything yet. 'How many nephews and nieces have you got?' she asked.

'Nine at the last count. I come from a large family.'

And yet he wasn't married himself. Zoe's curiosity grew. 'Are they local?'

He shook his head. 'I'm from Newcastle originally. Both my sisters have stayed in that area. My brother lives in Australia—my parents are out visiting him now. We keep in touch but they all have young families and I'm busy and...' He shrugged.

'I'm jealous,' said Zoe. And she was, more than he could guess. She could think of nothing better than to have a large supportive family. A noise suggestive of disaster from the living room recalled her. 'Jamie, what are you...?'

He followed her. 'I should be getting back to the Centre. Thanks for... You've changed things!'

Jamie had upended a box of toys. Small cars, plastic give-aways and a dismantled Lego set were scattered on the carpet. Zoe groaned. What would Connor *think*? 'Yes,' she said dis-tractedly. 'I had to shift the chairs to get my sofa and table in.

I've put the little table that was here upstairs in my bedroom.'
She looked up and saw his austere expression. Oh, help. Wasn't
she supposed to have moved things? 'Look, I'm sorry, I...'

But he was going. 'Thanks for the scone. It was very nice.
You be careful, young man, don't stand on the gate again until
it's mended.'

'All right,' said Jamie absently.

At the patio door, Connor turned. Just for a moment he
stood silent, looking at her. She saw his eyes flick a glance at
her legs, rest on the curve of her breasts, then look at her face.
She couldn't read his expression. Annoyance? Desire, maybe?
But not lust. She got the impression that he was irritated by
their intrusion into his life, but he was also aware of her
body—and its potential. She felt herself colouring, and with
that came the urge to fight back. He was arousing thoughts in
her that she neither liked nor wanted. She needed to make him
aware that she was a person in her own right. That she had
her own feelings, which might not be the same as his.
Whatever his feelings might be.

'I won't shake hands,' she said. 'Too much wooden furniture in this house for sparks jumping around.'

'That was simple physics,' he said. 'The conditions are different now. Goodbye, Zoe.'

Zoe watched him go. It really did look as though he was
fighting the attraction just as much as she was. Good. So why,
in the name of all stupid things, did that leave her feeling very
unsatisfied indeed?

# CHAPTER TWO

CONNOR strode furiously back to his house. She'd changed the living room! She'd filled it with clutter. She'd moved his favourite armchair—all right, maybe it *was* a bit tatty, that was why his sisters had banished it to the coach house—from where he could relax and watch the sunset, over to the far corner of the room where he wouldn't be able to see anything! The fact that he'd rented the place to her so he wouldn't be doing any sunset-watching for a while was irrelevant.

And she'd taken the little Regency table upstairs! Did she know how valuable that was? What if she'd damaged the legs getting it up the narrow staircase? So thoughtless!

Connor had another spurt of rage as he remembered the half-unpacked boxes lying everywhere. Where were her risk-assessment skills? The little boy could easily catch himself on one and sustain an injury. And what a thing to wear—*Ask me: I might*—what sort of signal did that give to a child? Blasted T-shirt didn't even fit properly.

As he entered his study he saw a light flashing on his computer; he had mail. A brief message from his sister. *Arabella has chicken pox and wants to talk to Uncle Connor. Skype her!*

Connor sighed. He wasn't in the mood to be a jolly uncle. Why couldn't they understand? He was fine on his own, fine until they forced him to remember what it was like being part of an affectionate family, reminding him of everything he'd sworn off for his own peace of mind. He typed, *Sorry, too busy to Skype. Will be in touch when things are easier.* But, on the point of hitting the send button, he reluctantly cancelled the email. He was a doctor and his niece was ill, so…

'Hello, Arabella,' he said, after dealing with the connections. 'Urgh! You've got the pox!'

His niece's spotty, mournful face broke into a gap-toothed grin as she looked out at him from the screen. 'We have! Micky's *covered* in them. And Mummy says she's sick of house arrest so we're coming to stay with you and play in your garden until they scab over.'

'You can't,' said Connor, horrified at the idea. 'I've…I've got tenants in the coach house. They've only just moved. It wouldn't be fair to give them chicken pox.'

Arabella's lower lip wobbled. 'Mummy,' she wailed, 'Uncle Connor is being horrible.'

'I heard,' said his sister's voice. The screen blurred as she sat down and lifted Arabella onto her lap. Her face was sceptical as she said, 'Tenants, Connor? Really?'

'Really,' he said, blessing Jo for the first time since she'd mooted the idea. 'The new midwife at the practice and her little boy. Jo arranged it. Zoe is an old friend of hers.' *Zoe.* Why should speaking her name aloud unsettle him?

'Zoe? Pretty name. Pretty face, too?'

'Helen, please stop trying to pair me up with every stray female who wanders across your radar. I've told you before that I'm fine on my own.'

'And I've told you that you aren't.'

Connor ground his teeth. This was why he rarely made contact unless he had to. 'Forget it,' he said. 'Apart from anything else, Zoe's husband died in a car crash not long ago.' Even if anyone looking less like a grieving widow he had yet to meet. The memory of her in those brief shorts, spilling out of her T-shirt as she cradled Jamie…

'Connor?' Helen leaned forward and gave her screen a sharp tap. 'Wretched computer made you look really weird for a moment. Honestly, if *this* dies as well as having chicken pox in the house, I'll go mad. It's the only thing keeping Arabella amused.'

Connor found his voice. 'One game of battleships, pet, and then I must get to evening surgery.' And he would turn the webcam off before he stood up. Much as he wanted to ignore his new tenant, the unexpectedly erotic memory of Zoe in shorts and a T-shirt had had a very unfortunate effect on his body.

Midwifery in the Derbyshire countryside was vastly different from midwifery in London. When making a home visit in the city, Zoe wouldn't dream of leaving her car unlocked or without checking that the windows were firmly closed. In certain areas she parked a quarter of a mile from the place she was visiting in case the locals wondered if midwives kept drugs in their vehicles.

High Peak Farm was different. Three days into her new life, she parked in a cobbled yard, stepped out of the car and for a minute took a deep breath and looked at the view. Woods and fields, not row after row of roofs. She left the car windows half open, knowing everything would be safe. Oh, she could learn to love it here.

Towards her came a smiling farmer, hand outstretched. 'Hi, I'm Luke Beskin. You must be the new midwife. You've moved up here from London.'

Jo had warned her that there was none of the anonymity of the city here. Everyone knew everyone else's business— and felt entitled to.

Zoe shook hands. 'Yes, I'm Zoe Hilton. Isn't this a lovely view?'

The farm was perched on the top of a hill. They could see fields in the valley below, and beyond that was the darker heather of the moors.

Luke nodded. 'I was born here. I look out every morning and think how good it is. Mind you, this is summer. Just wait till winter. Visit in snow time and I'll have to fetch you up the lane in the tractor.'

Zoe laughed. 'I'll look forward to that.' And she meant it.

She was visiting Paula, Luke's wife, who was thirty-one weeks pregnant and had asked if possible to have a home delivery. Jo had told her it was practice policy to go along with home deliveries—even for first babies—if there was no apparent danger.

Zoe had checked her notes, had found that the previous midwife had thought it quite possible, and that so far there were no contra-indications. But she still needed to see Paula and her environs for herself.

Paula Beskin was waiting in a ground floor room that had been turned into a bedroom. She was a pleasant and obviously sensible girl, resting on top of the bed. She cradled her bump with that expression Zoe had seen so often on a primigravida's face—a mixture of happiness, anticipation and slight anxiety. Her skin had the rich tone that often came with pregnancy. Zoe noticed a door to an en suite shower room. Good. All satisfactory so far.

She introduced herself and sat by the bed to have a chat. Medical stuff could come in a minute. It was important to get to know Paula as a person before treating her as a patient.

'I've been coming to High Peak Farm since I was little,' Paula told her. 'Luke and I were childhood sweethearts but it's a standing joke that I only married him so I could live here.' She smiled, to show she was kidding. 'Now I want to have my baby here. I don't want any of our children born in some anonymous city hospital ward with buildings and traffic all around us. I want to nurse them where we can look out and see the farmlands and the valley.'

Zoe couldn't help smiling at her enthusiasm. She suspected when the time came Paula wouldn't much care where the birth was as long as it was over with quickly and safely. 'We'll arrange it if it's possible,' she said diplomatically. 'But you do understand…?'

'If there's a medical reason why you want me in hospital, I'll be there as fast as Luke can drive. The baby comes first.'

'Good,' said Zoe, relieved. 'Lie flat and let's have a look at you.'

It was a routine inspection. Questions about how Paula felt her baby moving. Blood pressure, pulse, urine test for leucocytes, protein and glucose. Then a physical inspection to feel the size, position, presentation and engagement of the baby. A listen to the baby's heart. All was well.

'So far you've been the perfect mum-to-be,' Zoe told her. 'Now, the EDD is another eight weeks, but babies have a habit of coming into the world in their own time. What do you need to look out for?'

'The first sign will probably be painful contractions which are regular, become more frequent and more painful,' recited Paula with a grin. 'They are not to be mistaken for Braxton Hicks contractions, which are irregular and not too painful. Phone the midwife when the interval is twenty minutes. If the waters break, phone the midwife at once. Oh, and don't panic.'

Zoe laughed. 'All right, you've done your homework. Just let me know in plenty of time. You've got my mobile number. Any time, day or night.'

'Right.' Shyly, Paula went on, 'I'm glad you're going to be my midwife. But I hear you've got a little boy. What happens if I ring in the middle of the night?'

The country grapevine again. How had Paula found out about Jamie so quickly? It was almost scary. 'Don't worry about it. Jo Summers, the practice manager, has organised things. She'll come over straight away, and then the school assistant in charge of the babysitting rota will start ringing round.'

'Shelley,' said Paula with a nod. 'I went to school with her. Bring your little boy to look round the farm after school one day if you like. Luke needs to get used to children. Though he's looking forward to having his own.'

'I'm sure he'll be a wonderful father. Now, any problem— just ring me. And I'll see you again in a couple of weeks.'

Zoe's first countryside home visit was over and she had enjoyed every minute of it. If they could all be like this, midwifery would be wonderful! She laughed at herself as she thought of the assorted cantankerous, ill-mannered or monosyllabic mums-to-be she had dealt with in her time. One brilliant visit and you forgot them all! Perhaps she would be all right in the country.

She stepped into the sunshine and reassured Luke that everything was going well. He handed her a box. 'Here's a dozen eggs, farmyard fresh. They'll make your little lad a big lad in no time.'

Zoe was impressed.

Another visit on her way home, then afternoon clinic before collecting Jamie from school. As she walked purposefully along the passage to her room, she saw Connor coming towards her. She felt her heart beat slightly faster, thought she detected an awkwardness in the way his step faltered for a second.

'Getting on all right?' he asked.

'Yes. I've just been to High Peak Farm *and* Buckley Netherton without getting lost,' she said with happy pride. 'I even avoided the collie who wanted to attack my tyres.'

His face broke into a surprising smile. 'It's an experience, isn't it? A few more weeks and you'll have forgotten how to work traffic lights or what a box junction looks like.'

'That's right! You were a city boy too! What made you move?'

Immediately the moment of intimacy was as if it had never been. 'Reasons,' he said curtly.

Zoe didn't stop to think. She put a hand on his arm. Anything to banish that bleak pain in his eyes. 'Would you go back? I'm curious.'

There was an eon of time when she wondered what had possessed her and when she belatedly realised that he was in a short-sleeved shirt and the skin of his forearm was warm and solid under her palm.

He took a deep breath. 'No. No, I wouldn't.'

'Me neither,' she said. 'Mind you, it *has* only been three days, and it *is* the height of summer…'

He laughed and the tension was broken. Zoe lifted her hand. 'My clinic calls.' Inside her room she sat down at her desk, her legs absurdly weak. 'Work,' she told herself sternly.

'Linda Brown?'

The wiry, short-haired woman standing in the doorway nodded, her eyes unfriendly. 'Am I going to have the same trouble with you as I did with the other midwife?' she demanded.

Zoe remained calm. 'Come and take a seat, Linda. Let me see; by your dates you are sixteen weeks pregnant.'

Another terse nod.

'And it's been two months since your last appointment. Have you been keeping well?'

'Fine. No thanks to *her*.'

'If you have a complaint, you should talk to the practice manager,' said Zoe peaceably. 'I'm just here to look after your well-being and the well-being of your baby.'

'She told me I couldn't run,' burst out Linda. 'I have to run. I have to stay fit. Otherwise I'll lose my place in the team!'

Zoe's eyes flicked to Linda's records, though she already

knew what they said. An athlete, a national level runner. One who didn't want to take a break, by the sound of it. 'Well, now, I don't like being at outs with my mums-to-be. What does your coach advise?'

'She moved away. We haven't got one at the moment. I do about a hundred miles a week. I can't just stop!'

Zoe swiftly ran through the options in her head. Fretting would be just as bad for Linda as too much exercise. They needed an expert here. 'Bear with me,' she said, dialling Jo's internal number. 'I'm new and I don't know all the doctors' specialities. Hi, Jo, sorry to bother you—who would be the best doctor to advise a pregnant athlete, please?'

Jo chuckled in her ear. 'I'll send someone along.'

While they waited, Zoe carried out her routine examination, frowning when she saw the woman's weight was well down. There was a knock, followed immediately by the door opening. Zoe looked around with a smile—and felt her mouth drop open. Connor! What made him an expert on athletes? And why should seeing him unexpectedly cause her heart to suddenly pound much too hard?

But he was introducing himself courteously and asking Zoe how he might help. Zoe took refuge in protocol and explained. Linda Brown looked as if Christmas had come early when Connor said straight away that yes, she must most certainly carry on regular training, although she might have to modify her routine. He then went on to ask about her current regime, her general health, her day job, whether she had family support.

Zoe took discreet notes, appreciating the way Connor was sliding in advice about sticking to weight-bearing activities, suggesting a course of action that would see Linda walking rather than running or jogging in her last trimester and also sounding her out about how she felt towards the baby and parenthood. Interposing her own instructions to eat proper meals,

Zoe wondered about that last line of questions. Maybe she was imagining it, but Connor seemed to be placing a lot of emphasis on establishing that Linda and her partner wanted the baby and that she didn't resent the new life inside her. For all his serious, pleasant air, he was making quite a point about making sure the runner wasn't going to compromise the health of the foetus. It was a good thing Linda was her last patient of the day—anyone still outside would be having a long wait.

Linda left much happier than when she'd arrived and promising to attend appointments more regularly in the future.

'A driven woman,' commented Connor, his hand on the door ready to go. His eyes were bleak.

'As long as she listens to advice, that's not a bad thing. Thank you for helping. How do you know so much about having children and—'

'I wasn't busy and it's my job,' he said, interrupting her. 'That reminds me—you're going over to the maternity unit at Sheffield hospital to get signed on and registered and so on?'

'Yes, Jo's taking me tomorrow.'

'She *was*. Now she's got a finance meeting and asked, as I was going over anyway to check on half a dozen of our patients, would I mind taking you instead.'

Something in his tone of voice made Zoe's hackles rise. 'And do you?' she asked tartly.

'Excuse me?'

'Do you mind? After all, I drove to Buckley from London. I found two outlying farms this morning. I'm quite sure I could drive another twenty miles to Sheffield without getting lost.'

'Of course I don't mind. It's just that Jo…' He broke off, passing a hand across his eyes. 'Forget it. I'm a bit tired, that's all. Can you be ready by nine tomorrow?'

And now he would think she got prickly over the least little thing. What on earth was the matter with her? 'I'll wait in reception,' she said. She thought ruefully that she knew what he'd been about to say. *It's just that Jo often has her own agenda.* Which she did. And throwing them together for the morning wasn't what you might call subtle. Zoe thought she might just have to have a word with her friend and ask her which part of *I am staying single for the rest of my life* she didn't understand. It wasn't until she was hurrying to fetch Jamie that she realised Connor had diverted her interest in his 'speciality' very neatly. She also wondered why he was so tired.

Connor leaned his forehead against the cool panes of his window. This was ridiculous. He was letting Zoe Hilton get under his skin. There was no reason whatsoever why any of the doctors at this practice shouldn't give a new midwife a lift to the hospital to oversee their registration, so why had he felt instantly manipulated when Jo made the request?

His was an upstairs office. He looked down at the familiar school playground without seeing it. He'd slept badly last night, plagued with snippets of dreams in which his nephews and nieces played around him calling him their favourite Uncle Connor, but that was no reason to have got irritated during a professional conversation. He did feel manipulated, though. When Jo had originally suggested that Connor might rent Zoe the coach house, she had described her friend as newly widowed, desperate to get away from the scene of her husband's car crash, in no fit state to make decisions on renting or buying houses. The impression she had given was of someone small and slight, battered, at the mercy of her memories. Was it any wonder he thought he'd been had? Zoe was *not* small and slight. She came up easily to his shoulder and she filled that uniform of hers extremely well. And she laughed. She had…vibrancy.

And she cared.

Connor didn't need any care in his life. He kept his family at a safe distance and his old friends on the end of sporadic emails. He liked his colleagues but none of them was close.

He was making a new quiet, self-contained life for himself. He enjoyed the work, liked the countryside, found nothing to disturb him. He knew he was not yet cured. He had seen too many patients who thought they were over an illness and plunged into their previous life without any thought of a period of recuperation. It always ended in disaster. And you didn't get over a severe case of Lyme disease that easily. He remembered the long weeks of lying in bed or sitting in a chair, unable to walk more than a few steps, unable to concentrate on anything. He wasn't going back to that. But he'd regained his former strength, was starting to pick up his old pastimes. He was building up his walking, doing some climbing—though his joints occasionally complained—even canoeing.

But there was being physically fit—and being emotionally fit. And no way was he the second. The illness—and the personal misery that followed it—had done more than injure his body. It had left him emotionally scarred. The fact that he was aware of this didn't make it any less true. Which was why he was determined to stay well away from anything—or anyone—that might set him back. Zoe attracted him, therefore she had the potential to hurt him. He needed to be very careful.

Happy shouts of children being released from school broke his reverie. Despite the bitter knowledge that he would never have any of his own, the sound always brought a tiny smile to his lips. He looked down into the playground. And there was Zoe again, chatting to one of the other mums. She'd unpinned her hair. It was a rich dark brown colour, its shine reminding him of the conkers he used to gather as a boy. Earlier it had been twisted up in some convenient way, but now it cascaded down below her shoulders just like it had yesterday. It made her seem free and untrammelled, not the efficient midwife who'd consulted him about a patient. If he was being fanciful, it seemed to suggest that at times she just liked to let things go.

Her little boy came out of the doorway, looked around uncertainly and then spotted her with what Connor thought was relief. She gave him a swift hug, took the piece of paper he showed her. Jamie pointed things out on it. Connor saw Zoe blot her eyes with her sleeve when he wasn't looking. Odd. What could he have drawn that made her cry?

Zoe had just put the potatoes on to boil when she became aware that Jamie's bike was still, the saddle empty. Heart in mouth, she dashed outside, only to stop as she saw her son sitting cross-legged on the path, watching Connor mend the gate.

She hid a smile. For a man who was so precise with his patients, he was making a decidedly amateur job of nailing a piece of wood across a couple of uprights. But he was talking to Jamie with nothing of the reserve he kept for her, telling him what the saw was for, explaining how trees were turned into planks, both of them speculating as to how nails might be made. Zoe went quietly back to the kitchen.

Ten minutes later there was an, 'Ow,' and a bitten-off curse from outside and suddenly Jamie was tugging Connor up the path.

'It's all right,' he was saying anxiously. 'Mummy's got plasters. They stop germs getting in. And you can draw smiley faces on them.'

Connor was dark red with embarrassment. 'It's only a splinter,' he muttered. 'I picked up the broken strut without looking.'

'Sit down and I'll get it out, then,' said Zoe, reaching for tweezers. 'Splinters are like paper cuts—the pain is out of all proportion to the size of the wound.'

Jamie hovered, distressed. Zoe gave Connor full marks for noticing this and distracting him. 'I like your pictures,' he said, nodding towards the fridge.

Zoe smiled as Jamie explained them to Connor. Today's

drawing was identical to the first, except for the addition of a broken gate and a new path leading off on the other side.

'He likes mapping out his surroundings,' she said. 'But he does tend to put in only the things that are of interest to him.'

'…and that's Daddy in Heaven,' finished Jamie.

Zoe was holding Connor's hand steady. She pulled out the splinter and continued to hold on, just for a moment. To her utter astonishment, he closed his fingers over hers in brief sympathy.

'That's done,' she said, and let go. She didn't want sympathy. It would be taking something for the wrong reason. 'A good wash and a dab of antiseptic and you'll be right as rain.'

'Thank you.' He looked at the pan bubbling on the stove and sniffed appreciatively. 'Something smells good.'

She chuckled. 'Fish fingers, new potatoes and peas. I'd offer to share, but fish fingers only come in packs of ten these days, and Jamie and I are really hungry.'

He laughed out loud. Zoe was truly amazed, contrasting the gravely interested doctor at the surgery with this amused man, carefree for one blinding second. It was *astonishing* how his whole bearing could lighten up like that. This was how he was supposed to be. Her amazement must have shown on her face because his laughter died as he met her eyes.

'I'll…um.…see you tomorrow morning, then,' he said.

'Sure.'

'I told you Mummy would make it better.' Jamie put his hand in Connor's.

For a moment, Zoe saw the total shock on Connor's face. *Please,* she thought, *please don't rebuff him.*

Connor looked down at the small hand tucked so confidently in his, then smiled ruefully and let Jamie trot down the path alongside him.

Zoe watched the pair of them, watched Connor jump on the strut of the gate to test it, and then keep a careful eye on Jamie as he did the same. She watched as he picked up his tools, said goodbye to her son and disappeared towards his own house. A nice man. So who had damaged him? Because somebody most certainly had.

# CHAPTER THREE

CONNOR came down the stairs to reception at precisely nine a.m. to find Zoe ready and waiting. In fact he'd already known she was there because he heard her voice when he was halfway down. Zoe's voice—try as he might not to admit it—was marvellous, low-pitched, musical and calming. He knew how important voices could be in medicine and could see that if a mum-to-be was having trouble giving birth then Zoe's voice would soothe her. That was if her smile hadn't done the job first. Connor paused on the bottom step, analysing it. The smile said that Zoe was happy and she wanted you to be happy too. The infuriating thing was that it worked. Meeting her in the corridor yesterday, he'd been awkward and she'd cheered him up. Yesterday evening he'd been downright embarrassed, and she'd made it no big deal. But he'd also seen moments of stillness in her—she was obviously still grieving for her husband. How could she simply put her own unhappiness aside?

Anyway, today they were doctor and midwife, professional colleagues getting a tedious bit of business over with. He walked through the swing doors in full control. 'Ready, Zoe?'

'Absolutely.' And she turned from laughing with the receptionists and her wide smile hit him squarely in the solar plexus.

\* \* \*

The trouble with car journeys was the air of forced intimacy. If you weren't careful, the enclosed space, the sense of being separate from the rest of the world, could turn into a confessional. Connor intended to be very careful indeed.

'How are you settling in at the coach house?' he asked, before she could get comfortable and start a topic of her own.

'It's perfect,' she said. 'Jamie loves the garden. We lived in a flat in London, so we had to spend a lot of time in the park. This is like having a mini-park of his own. The only thing that would make it more perfect as far as he's concerned would be a set of swings and bouncy seesaws—but I told him you can't have everything, and we're going over to Jo's at the weekend, where he can play on their outdoor equipment.'

Swings and seesaws? Connor had a momentary stab of guilt, but she was still talking.

'The coach house itself is just lovely. I can see once Jamie gets to be a lanky teenager leaving huge anoraks and size twelve trainers everywhere it might not be big enough, but just now it's exactly the right size for one and a bit. It kind of wraps itself around you.'

'It does!' agreed Connor, startled to have his own feelings put into words. 'I thought the same thing as soon as I first walked through the door. I was ready to give the estate agent the money for it on the spot.'

Zoe chuckled. 'But then you saw the big house and couldn't resist the two-for-one deal?'

'Oh, I'd already seen that. Jo put me onto it and the family nagged me into buying it. I'm still convinced it was less for me and more so they'd have a useful holiday home in the Peak District.'

'Why buy the coach house as well, then?'

'So I'd have somewhere to escape to,' he said feelingly. 'And also because I didn't want neighbours.'

There was a split-second pause. 'Oh,' said Zoe.

Connor could have banged his head on the steering wheel. This was what he'd meant by a confessional. He'd have to remember Zoe was appallingly easy to talk to. 'Neighbours not of my own choosing, I mean.'

'But—you didn't choose us.'

'Jo did. Her judgement is generally sound.' Had he said enough to cover his rudeness? 'What made you go into mid-wifery?' he asked, changing the subject.

She smiled again but, glancing sideways at her, he thought there was a touch of sadness. 'Do you want the short answer or the long one?'

A road sign flashed by. Sheffield: sixteen miles. 'The long one,' he said.

She wrinkled her nose. 'Okay; you asked for it. I said the other day that my father died when I was quite young. It was a terrible blow to my mother—she'd been completely bound up in him. He was in the army, so we'd moved from base to base every few years. Looking back on it now, she hadn't had the chance to make close friends any more than I did, but it didn't matter to her because Dad was her whole world.'

Connor glanced sideways again, catching the nuance in her voice even if she didn't realise it was there. She'd been lonely.

'I wasn't unhappy that Mum was leaning on me. I just knew there was more to life. Girls at school would talk about bowling, or discos or kissing boys in the back row of the cinema—and I didn't have anything similar to relate to. But then, when I was fifteen, the school I was at arranged for me to spend time in a hospital on a Work Experience scheme.'

She looked at him, her face lighting up, and he felt a strange thud in his chest. 'Oh, Connor, I came alive! I loved it—the intimacy, the teamwork, the feeling that I was helping, the knowledge that I was needed by people other than my mother. We moved around the departments and one day I was observing in the Delivery Suite when there was a birth. The moment I saw that tiny, new little person emerging, I knew what I wanted to do with my life. The rush of feelings shown by the mum when the baby was first placed in her arms, the tears of the watching father, the broad grins on the faces of the midwife and nursing staff—they were like rain in the desert, completely missing in my own life. I wanted to bring that joy. I wanted to live, not just exist. I wanted to be part of it. So I decided to train as a midwife.'

'I needn't ask if it's been everything you expected.'

'More,' she said simply. 'Sometimes it's kept me sane.'

*Sane?* Connor looked at her sharply, but was distracted by a wave of red brake lights ahead. He frowned. There was only half a mile to go—they should have missed the rush hour—what was going on?

He slowed. There must have been an accident at the roundabout. As the car came to a complete stop, his previous fears were realised as Zoe said, 'Anyway, that's my story; what about you? Have you always wanted to be a GP?'

As she asked the question, Zoe saw Connor's face tighten. She saw him look at the stationary traffic in front of them, saw his eyes flick to the mirrors to the queue backing up behind.

He sighed. 'Nearly. I entered medicine intending to be a GP. Did my first six years and then started the GP training programme. You know it, I'm sure—four six-month periods in hospital in various GP-friendly specialities. Several of my pals in the climbing club were doing surgery, so I chose that as one of the options to give me a different perspective. And I found I liked it—and I was good at it. The hospital persuaded me I shouldn't waste my talent, so I began training to be a surgeon.'

Listening to him, Zoe suspected he'd forgotten she was there. He wasn't just telling her his story now, he was re-living it. Perhaps re-examining his choices.

Reflectively, he said, 'Climbing skills help you be a good surgeon. You learn never to panic, never to move too quickly, to concentrate on the job you're doing. You feel the same way when you're balanced on two tiny ridges over a six hundred foot drop as you do when you're about to cut into living tissue. Aware of the dangers but not nervous, not afraid. Focused.'

Zoe was fascinated. Not just with the story, but what it told her about Connor. This was what she'd seen as he'd walked through the theatre on her first morning. That complete command. 'What happened? Why aren't you still doing it?'

'I contracted Lyme disease.' The words were quiet, but she could feel the carefully controlled emotion behind them. 'My consultant—who was a friend of mine—told me cheerfully that it was one of the worst cases ever seen in England.'

She frowned. 'It rings a bell. Remind me.'

'It's a bacterial disease. Common in some US states, but few lay people over here have ever heard of it. It wasn't even named until 1975. For the vast majority of sufferers it's just like a bad dose of flu with a nasty skin rash. For the unlucky ones—the ones who don't show any symptoms to begin with so they aren't treated with the right antibiotics straight away—basically the bacteria melts down the nervous system.'

'You were one of the unlucky ones?'

'Yes.' He was silent for a moment. 'I didn't work for a year. I already knew—before Mick confirmed it—that, even fully recovered, I would never be a top rank surgeon again. The pressure on me would be too intense. So I came here to train for my third year as a GP registrar. And now I'm a fully-fledged general practitioner who is also registered on the local health authority's minor surgery list.'

The car had fugged up. It was as if they were in a place separate from day-to-day living. Zoe could feel Connor's pain, could almost taste the crumbling of his dreams. 'That's the bravest thing I've ever heard,' she said, humbled.

His head whipped round, his dark blue eyes astonished. 'Brave?'

She held his gaze. 'Going from the top of your tree to a little way up the trunk of another one. Changing direction instead of throwing things around the room and screaming. Yes, I think that's brave.' Neil wouldn't have done it. Neil would have picked up a bottle and settled down with it for the rest of his life. But Connor wasn't Neil.

Connor scrubbed jerkily at the condensation on the windows. 'There was—actually—quite a lot of screaming,' he muttered.

And Zoe would have bet the last pound in her purse that no one had heard it. As the traffic started moving again she reflected that there was a considerable amount more to Dr Connor Maitland than met the eye. The question was, even if he'd let her, did she want to compromise her own no-intimacy status by probing deeper?

It had, thought Zoe, been another good day. Connor had introduced her to the manager of the maternity unit, established her credentials, got her signed in to the system. Then he'd done his patient visits while she was shown around and inducted. He'd been a bit quiet on the way back—she had the feeling one of his patients was troubling him—but they had stuck to medical matters and she'd thanked him for the lift and they'd gone to their respective clinics. And now the potatoes and hard-boiled eggs were cooling down ready for a nice salad and she'd taken her laptop outside to look up Lyme disease in the sunshine while Jamie rode his bike up and down the path.

'Hi,' called Connor's voice. 'Am I disturbing you?'

Zoe hastily shut the machine down. 'No. Is something wrong? Is Jamie being too noisy?'

He was standing on his path looking uncomfortable again.

'Not at all. I just wondered… What you said about swings in the park…'

Jamie came to a halt by the gate and looked at Connor hopefully.

Connor took a deep breath and opened the gate. 'I'll start again. First, I thought Jamie might like to ride along *my* path now and again, because it's longer and he won't have to keep turning round. And second… Well, it's pure guilt, really. Come along here and I'll show you.'

Jamie shifted his hopeful gaze to Zoe. 'Can we, Mum?'

Zoe stood up, tugging down the hem of her shorts and feeling flustered. At least she was wearing a slightly less re-vealing T-shirt today. Mind you, looking at Connor's own T-shirt and chinos, she wondered why she was bothered. Thin material outlined the muscles of his thighs and arms as he ushered them through the gate. The plain lines emphasised the broadness of his shoulders. The absence of a belt showed his flat belly. Why was this man not spoken for? Connor Maitland was *so* something else.

Jamie's trainer wheel caught on the gatepost. She bent down to free it just as Connor said, 'Backwards a bit, then forwards again, lad.'

She hurriedly jerked away before Jamie ran over her fingers. As she straightened up, Connor met her eyes.

'Sorry,' he said. 'Too many cooks. Didn't mean to interfere.'

'No, yours…' She forced herself to say it. 'Yours was the better suggestion. Mothers are inclined to fix things out of habit rather than get kids to solve problems for themselves.' It was true and she meant it—it was just odd, somebody else doing it for her son.

'That's magnanimous of you.' Zoe saw Connor's gaze travel down over her T-shirt, her shorts, her legs. He looked away almost immediately, but she thought he'd liked what he'd seen. It made her feel strangely shaky.

'Mummy!' Jamie had come to a dead stop where the path divided to go either up to Connor's house or down to a small wooded area. His eyes were huge in his face. 'Oh, Mummy, come and see! There's swings, Mummy! And a slide and a little house!'

In his excitement he'd forgotten how to turn the bike. His sandals were getting tangled up with the pedals. Connor loped forward, laughing.

'Steady, lad. There you go.'

He lifted him off and Jamie ran into the little copse. By the time Zoe reached the abandoned bike he had scrambled onto a swing and was energetically pumping himself backwards and forwards.

Zoe looked around in wonder. It was a perfect pocket play area. There were two swings, a climbing frame with a slide attachment and a child-sized plastic cottage with a sandpit for a garden. Forest bark—obviously freshly laid—was spread thickly over the ground. The sharp, pungent smell stung her nostrils. 'Connor, what is this?'

'It was all left by the previous owner. My nieces and nephews adore it. They all come for a week's holiday every summer.'

'That must make it crowded.'

'I move into the coach house. Alone.'

Zoe looked at him in amazement. He didn't stay to be with them? But he was great with children!

'Anyway,' he said gruffly, 'after what you said in the car, I gave my gardener a ring and asked him to renew the bark. If Jamie would like to, he can play here any time.'

Zoe didn't know what to say. It was an incredibly generous gesture from a man who had bought an entire coach house because he hadn't wanted neighbours. 'Thank you. Of course he'd love it. I'd…I'd have to be with him, mind.'

'You're more than welcome.' He indicated the curved wooden benches around the edge of the enclosure. 'Do you want to sit?'

She did. 'Connor, this is really nice of you.' *She'd be welcome? What did he mean?*

'I have my nice moments. Is that your phone?'

She blinked and realised that her pocket was vibrating. It was part of her job—calls could come any time, day or night. She focused on the display. Jo's number, so it could be either business or pleasure.

He made to stand up, move away so she could take her call in privacy. She put her hand on his arm, indicating that he should stay. It would have been incredibly rude to drive him out of his own garden. And again there was a definite thrill as her palm met his skin.

Jo sounded strangely unconfident. 'Are you doing anything tonight, Zoe?'

*Only looking up Lyme disease and staving off inappropriate thoughts.* 'Nothing special. Why?'

'I need to visit someone and I'd like to take an impartial friend along who just happens to be a midwife. Can you come over?'

'Sure. But what about Jamie? How long are we going to be?'

'I don't know. Possibly quite a while. Bring him here. Sam can look after him with ours. We've got a spare bed.'

'Okay. I'll be there in half an hour or so.' She rang off, gnawing her lip. Of course she had to help Jo where she could but she didn't like the idea of uprooting Jamie, even just for a night, when he was trying to settle into their new home.

Connor watched Zoe's face change. 'Problem?' he asked when she finished.

'Sort of. I've got a call-out and I'm to take Jamie over to Jo's. He gets on all right with her girls but he hasn't even had his tea yet and he's only just used to settling in his new bedroom here and…' She stood up. 'Oh, well. No point dithering over what can't be helped.'

'Wait.' Blast. Connor had a short wrestle with himself,

wondering why all good deeds backfired. He didn't want this. He'd extended the invitation to the play dell purely because he had it and they didn't, and because there wasn't enough room for the kid to work off his energy at home. He didn't want to do what he was about to offer. He was a landlord, not a childminder! But how could he not when Jamie was so obviously happy, beaming at them as if life could hold no more as he threw himself backwards and forwards on the swing? 'I'm not on call this evening,' he heard himself say. 'It seems a shame to interrupt Jamie's routine. Would you like me to babysit? He could play here for a bit longer, then I could feed him, put him to bed, read him a bedtime story. I've done it on occasion for my nieces and nephews. I'm quite reliable.'

Zoe looked at him, open-mouthed and astounded. Connor wasn't surprised. He couldn't have made his offer sound more reluctant if he'd tried. He attempted a grin. 'Just this once,' he added, as if that might make it better.

She gave a wary smile. 'Thanks, but I couldn't possibly impose. Jamie, we've got to—'

It had only been a small smile on Connor's face, but as Zoe started to refuse his offer she saw it disappear, to be replaced by the bleak expression she had seen too often. Suddenly and unexpectedly, her heart flipped and she changed her mind. Deep inside, she knew she could trust him with Jamie. 'Oh, dear, look at him,' she said. 'Happy as a lark. If you really don't mind, I would be ever so grateful if you'd babysit. Jamie's been a bit…unused to people for a while but he's really taken to you. I don't think he'll give you any trouble.'

To her relief, Connor's face relaxed. 'That's settled, then. I need to grab a couple of things. Do you want to come and have a quick look at the house? Check me out?'

Zoe called Jamie and they walked up with him. Connor offering to babysit was the last thing she had expected. He hardly knew them, she was renting the house that he'd wanted to keep to himself, and the first thing Jamie had done was to break his gate! And yet…and yet, deep down, she knew perfectly well that there could easily be something between them if they let it start, let it grow. She tripped and he took her arm. Even though her mind was in turmoil, she was aware of the warmth of his hand on her bare skin. In another life she might have wanted that warmth to spread all over her body. But she wasn't in another life. She was right here, right now and, however her body felt about his, could she really trust her son to a man she'd only met a few days ago? A man who'd been uneasy about offering this favour.

Things are happening too quickly, she thought, hurrying with him. It was as if she was being taken on a journey without knowing where the end would be. She hated that. It had happened too many times before. But at least Connor was being purposeful, where Neil had been mercurial. There was a difference.

Connor's house was big. It was built in the same grey stone as the coach house and she guessed it was about a hundred years old.

They entered the house through French windows and walked quickly through what was obviously his living room. Zoe couldn't help slowing as she looked round. You could tell a lot about a person from their choice of furnishings. What did this room tell her about Connor?

It was a very spare room, a very male room. The pictures on the white walls were photographs of mountain scenes, of rivers, of climbers, all grinning for the camera even though they were only perilously attached to sheer rock-faces. There was a rich red Persian carpet on the polished floor but not much furniture—and what there was, was modern. She thought that the large mahogany fireplace, beautifully polished, was crying out for a set of family photographs. Or anything, really. This room desperately needed a woman's touch. And the room felt unused.

*Stop it. Stop thinking like that. No more relationships. Not ever. I don't trust them and I don't trust the feelings they raise in me.*

He realised she'd stopped following and came back. 'Don't tell me. You're thinking this room needs flowers and ornaments and scatter cushions.'

The tone was deadpan, but the astonishing thought that he might be teasing her was beguiling. 'It's very rude to read a person's mind like that,' she said reprovingly.

'The house is mostly self-defence. Too cosy and the family would be over more often.'

He was leading her through an equally minimalist hall and together they entered what was obviously Connor's study. Zoe could see at a glance that this was where he really lived. It was a room for working, reading, listening to music or just sitting. It was a comfortable room, lived in, slightly untidy. Two walls were covered with bookshelves. Against a third wall was a roll-top desk with a computer station to one side. Large windows looked out onto the garden and in the centre of the room was a massive easy chair with a stool to rest your feet on. A room made for masculine comfort. One man's masculine comfort. There wasn't a place for anyone extra. The only out of place touch was a defiantly girly pin-board crowded with children's photos and home-made birthday cards.

'Present?' said Zoe with a grin.

'How did you guess?'

Jamie was looking at the cards. 'To Uncle Connor with lots of love. Is that you?'

'Yes. My niece Arabella likes drawing pictures, just like you.' Connor picked up a file and a sweater from the back of his chair. Then he murmured, 'Zoe, shouldn't you ask Jamie first?'

'I doubt it's necessary. Jamie, I've got to go out so would you like to have Dr Maitland look after you and put you to bed?'

Jamie beamed. 'Does that mean I can go on the swings again?'

Zoe smiled. 'If you ask nicely.'

'Hooray.' He grabbed Connor's hand. 'Come on, Uncle Connor.'

*Uncle Connor?* Zoe followed, startled. She wasn't sure she was quite ready for that!

# CHAPTER FOUR

'SORRY to drag you out like this,' said Jo as Zoe got out of the car. She opened the rear door. 'We'll just get Jamie settled and then... Where is he?'

Zoe straightened her uniform unnecessarily. 'Connor was showing us his play area when you rang, so he offered to babysit.'

A wide smile appeared on Jo's lips. 'Fabulous.'

Zoe ignored her. It wasn't fabulous at all. Distinctly unsettling was more like it. 'Where are we going?'

'To see a friend of mine. We'll go in my car. Lock your bag in the boot of yours, then no one can accuse us of interfering.'

'Are you meddling again, Jo?'

'Visiting a poorly friend isn't meddling. Get in; I'll tell you as we go. Barbara Reagan used to be one of our receptionists, worked for us straight from school. Lovely girl. Quiet, but always helpful. Anyway, she married Roy, who she'd known for years.' Jo hesitated, choosing her words. 'He's good-looking, bit of a Jack-the-lad, and was brought up in a family where the man's always the boss.'

'Go on,' said Zoe. She'd come across that sort of chap before.

'Roy came to the surgery one day in a very belligerent mood demanding a sick note. Sam wouldn't give it to him. Said there was nothing wrong with him that doing without beer for a day or two wouldn't cure. Roy went ballistic, told Barbara she was leaving right there and then, and hustled her out.'

'Poor woman,' murmured Zoe. She knew what it was like being at the whim of a more dominant partner.

'A week later she resigned. Said she loved Roy and she knew he loved her, so she was doing the harmonious thing and getting a job at his firm instead. It must have worked, because she was pregnant soon after. She was still registered with us, but Roy always came with her to the appointments and picked fights incessantly with the midwife, telling her all the advice was rubbish.'

'I know the style. Don't tell me—his mother had fourteen kids and worked until she dropped each one and none of this namby-pamby vitamins and bed-rest.'

Jo grinned. 'That's the sort of thing. The birth was difficult. Roy objected to the follow-up care—said it wasn't necessary—and signed them both on with another practice.' Jo sniffed. 'I'm not being unprofessional when I say we're picking up a lot of their patients. Anyway, Barbara was pregnant again after three months. Last thing she needed. Fortunately, it was an easier birth this time.'

Zoe looked at her friend's profile as she pulled up outside a pleasant terraced house. 'Jo, she's with another practice. We can't go in there.'

Jo's lips were set in a line. 'She was one of ours! Part of the team. I've kept in touch and when I spoke to her this evening she sounded at the end of her tether. Said she couldn't cope with the babies, her doctor didn't care and all Roy wanted was his tea on the table at six o'clock and to go out to the pub with his mates every night. I know what I think the matter is—I want a friendly second opinion.'

Zoe sighed. Only too often medical and social work were mixed up. It was a case of doing what you could and hoping other professionals were suitably caring. 'As a friend, then,' she said.

The front door wasn't locked. Jo walked straight in, shouting, 'Barbara! It's me, Jo Summers. I've got a friend with me.'

There was no answer, just the crying of a very young child.

Zoe followed Jo. The living room showed that it had been decorated by someone with an eye for colour and line. There were glass vases with silk flowers in them, photographs of a smiling couple. But the place was a mess. Papers and baby clothes on the floor, a general air of neglect. Zoe wasn't surprised. The first few months after having a baby were tiring. And two babies, so close together, would be hard indeed.

Barbara was slumped in a chair, the crying infant on her lap. The older child was lying in a cot, wailing in sympathy. As they entered, Barbara looked up but neither smiled nor spoke.

It was a situation Zoe recognised at once. 'Baby blues,' she murmured. 'How much time have we got?'

Jo grinned broadly. 'I knew it. And I was hoping you'd suggest that deep-relaxation technique of yours. We've got time. I'll put the kids to bed. You work on Barbara.'

'Ahem. I'm not working, remember? I'm talking to her as a nice new relaxing friend.'

Barbara showed no objection to handing over her child. Zoe knelt by her chair, considering her white face, the eyes puffy with tears. 'First we have to calm you down,' she said. 'Lie back, shut your eyes, rest your hands on your knees. Now breathe in through your nose, as deeply as you can.' Zoe put her hand on Barbara's abdomen. 'I want you to feel the air here—not in your chest but here, lower down. Okay?' A moment later she felt the swell that indicated that Barbara was doing as she was told. 'Now hold it a minute…now breathe out as quickly as you can, through both mouth and nose.' Again, Barbara was obedient. 'Good. Now do exactly the same again. In through the nose, as deeply as you can, feel your belly swell…good.'

After a few breathing cycles, Zoe thought her technique was starting to work. 'Now keep your eyes shut, stay lying in your chair and we're going to relax you even further. Put your feet together, press them hard against each other until you can feel the muscles in your legs ache. Right? They're aching? Now relax the muscles in your legs. You know where they are now.'

Zoe took Barbara through all her major muscle groups, tightening and then relaxing them in turn. The aim was to have a completely relaxed body. It was important to have the right voice for this, and luckily Zoe knew she had it. Soon Barbara was much calmer, which meant that her pulse and blood pressure would be nearer normal. 'Now you're just going to be calm for a while,' she murmured. 'Don't think anything, don't do anything, just let life pass you by.'

She waited a minute, saw that Barbara's face looked happier, fewer worry lines. 'Think of a time in your past when you were perfectly happy and perfectly calm. A holiday. Or a day with a friend. Or just sitting in your garden. Remember that time?'

'Yes,' Barbara said after a moment. 'Roy and I went to Filey to a caravan. It was warm and we sat all week by the swimming pool. It was lovely.'

'Remember how you felt then. Remember the peace. In a moment you can open your eyes and we can talk.'

'Right,' said Barbara.

Half an hour later Jo put her head round the door, saw a relaxed Barbara sitting in her chair drinking tea with Zoe and looking brighter. 'Kids are in bed and we ought to be going,' she said. 'It wouldn't be a good idea if Roy found us here.'

'I'm going to tell him you've been.' Even Zoe was surprised at how firm Barbara sounded. 'I'm just as entitled to friends as he is. Jo, thanks for bringing Zoe round. I've been so tired I just couldn't think straight. I feel a lot better and I know what I have to do. Roy won't like it, but I can keep calm and tell him what I've decided. I want to sign back on with you. He does love me really; he'll agree. You looked after me far better than the doctor I'm going to now. Will you have me back as a patient?'

'You do ask daft questions,' said Jo, giving her a hug.

Zoe felt Jo's eyes on her as they walked out to the car. 'What did you do? How did you work that miracle?'

'I just showed her the relaxation technique that always works for me, and then I mentioned that I was sure Roy loved her, but in the wrong way. And that if she stood up to him quietly but firmly they'd both be happier.'

'Right,' said Jo. 'And I suppose she wasn't in any sort of semi-hypnotic state at the time?'

'Absolutely not,' said Zoe. 'Just very, very tired. There's a lot of work to be done yet. As soon as she's a signed-on patient of the Centre I can go round officially and see her again. We can probably persuade her to take the extra help she's been offered, which Roy turned away.'

They were driving down Buckley's main street. Zoe gazed out at the War Memorial surrounded by banks of flowers, at the sixteenth century church just beyond, at the shops, different shapes and sizes, not one long boring row. She felt happy here; this was a calming place, she felt at home. And she thought she had just done a good job. It was ironic that the one person whose problems she'd never been able to fix was herself.

Ahead she saw a shop, the Buckley Wine Store, and she had an idea. 'Jo, can you pull in a minute? I can't offer Connor money for babysitting Jamie, but I could get him a bottle of wine to show how grateful I am. Do you know what he likes?'

'Heavy oaky reds. Rioja or something similar.' Jo looked at her. 'What are you going to do if he offers to share it with you?'

'You told me he didn't like socialising.'

'Even so, it would be an idea to think about your answer before he asks the question, love.'

Zoe didn't want to think about it. It wouldn't happen. She would give Connor the wine; he would say thank you and go home, they would both breathe a sigh of relief. She went into the shop and asked the young man behind the counter if he had a good Rioja. He obviously took his job seriously. He fetched her three bottles. 'These two are both good wines, good value,' he said, lining them up on the counter. He placed his hand on the third bottle. 'This wine is superlative, well worth the extra money. For someone special, is it?'

'Not really,' she said. 'Yes, I'll have that bottle.' She looked at the gift bags that held just one bottle and had a variety of messages on the side. *For the Man in my Life.* Oh, no. Not ever again. Zoe decided plain paper was best.

When she got back in the car, Jo pulled down the wrapping and looked at the label. 'He'll like that,' she said approvingly, 'but he might think we're paying you too much. Do you want a coffee before you head off?'

'I ought to get back to Jamie.'

'Of course,' said Jo. She smiled.

'What?' asked Zoe.

'Nothing.'

'I'm back,' called Zoe as she opened the back door, then got a shock as she saw Connor sitting at his ease at her kitchen table, reading the *Buckley Gazette*. It gave her an odd feeling. He looked so comfortable there, as if he belonged. As if he was at home. Which he was, of course, in a way. But she'd forgotten how nice it was to come home after a call to a friendly presence. It took her right back to the old days before Neil went off the rails. For a moment she couldn't speak, drowning in a whirlpool of memories. *Why hadn't she seen the warning signs before it was too late? Why hadn't they talked it through when he first started to change?*

Connor looked up. 'All done? Did you manage to do what Jo wanted?'

'I think so,' she said, pulling herself together. 'How was Jamie? Did he cause you any trouble?'

'We had a great time. He had another go on the swings and then we played football. We turned his salad into a face and he ate every bit. We also discovered a couple more of those scones of yours. He had his bath, a bedtime story and fell asleep almost instantly. I told him you'd go up the minute you arrived home. I'll be on my way.'

'Wait.' Zoe was disoriented, beset by conflicting thoughts. On the one hand, she knew from experience that now she had started, she'd worry over every detail of her and Neil's life until she pinpointed something she'd said or done that had turned him bad. Or something she'd *not* said or done when she should. But if she asked Connor to stay so that she wasn't alone and could break the destructive-thought cycle, he could easily take the invitation the wrong way.

He stretched his arms above his head. It made him seem larger than ever in her tiny kitchen. He had a faint smile on his face, so he really must have had a good time with Jamie. It was another side to him. Who would have thought the reserved Dr Maitland would enjoy playing scrappy football with little children?

'I'll only be a second,' she said quickly. 'You don't need to rush off, do you?'

He hesitated. 'Not straight away.' He indicated the paper. 'I'll carry on studying stock prices at the local market. They're important round here. It helps with small talk for my patients.'

She felt oddly breathless as she went upstairs. She looked at the sleeping Jamie, kissed his cheek, smoothed his hair, pulled up his sheet. He was lovely! Then she went into her own bedroom, slipped out of her uniform and hesitated. What to put on instead? Not shorts, that was for sure. She'd seen the way Connor looked at her in shorts. Jeans and a blue silk top. And just the quickest moment in front of the mirror to brush her hair, to dab on a touch of make-up. It made her feel less vulnerable.

He folded the paper as she came back in. She caught the flash of appreciation in his eyes as he took in her outfit. Was the V-neck just a little too low?

She wasn't sure what to say so she simply took the bottle from where she had left it on the worktop. 'In London the babysitting rate is exorbitant. This is a small thank you.'

He shook his head. 'I don't need thanking. I meant it when I said I enjoyed myself.'

She shook her own head in turn. 'I'm glad, but I always pay my debts. If you don't accept this bottle, we'll have to haggle over whether it should be six or seven pounds an hour. It would be undignified, don't you think?'

He looked at the bottle and whistled at the label. 'This is a very generous present. I can't take it, Zoe. Keep it for a special occasion.'

'I don't have special occasions. It might lie in the cellar for years.'

'At least it would be there when you needed it.'

She chuckled. She'd missed normal adult conversation at home. But she still felt guilty that he'd spent some of his precious off-duty time looking after her son. 'Have you had any kind of food yet?' The invitation slipped from her mouth before she had a chance to consider it. It wasn't just that she didn't want to be alone—it was his comfortable presence in her kitchen and the fact that when he forgot to be wary he was good company. And if the comfortable presence had a casually muscular body, a mop of dark hair, a face that hid so much and yet could melt her with a smile, so what? There was never going to be anything in it. She'd been too badly scarred by Neil to want to repeat the experience. Besides which, she had Jamie to look after for the next ten years or so; she wasn't going to do anything that might mess *him* up, like starting a new relationship so quickly.

Connor paused before replying. 'I haven't eaten, no. I've got vegetable soup that I made yesterday and I was going to have a sandwich with it.'

She had a small moment of wonder that he made his own soup, followed by a disturbingly appealing domestic vision of him cooking in his kitchen. She cleared her throat. 'I bought some really gorgeous ham from that butcher on the High Street yesterday. Would you like to stay for a small meal? Ham and grown-up salad? You'd be very welcome.'

The corner of his mouth twitched. 'What's grown-up salad?'

She grinned. 'The same as Jamie had earlier, but we get to have dressing on it.'

'Difficult to turn down an offer like that.' She'd made him smile. He glanced at her a moment longer, as if he was trying to work something out. 'Are you sure there's enough?'

'I'm sure.'

'Then yes, please. And if you find me a corkscrew, we can have a glass each of this wine.'

*But it's not a special occasion.* The words nearly tumbled out. She compressed her lips, horrified. Because if she had said them and he'd said, *It could be*, then she'd have a conversation to face that she really didn't want to even contemplate tonight. But Connor's dark blue eyes were friendly and casual, so she waved him towards the second drawer down. It would be okay. They were two adults who had both come through pain and who weren't about to get hurt again.

After he had opened the wine and left it to breathe, he split and buttered the wonderful wholemeal rolls from the baker Jo had told her about. She protested that he didn't have to. He retaliated that he would feel awkward sitting doing nothing. It was a very mild obstinacy, but Zoe thought it wouldn't take much to turn it into full-blown intransigence. It felt weirdly intimate to be making a meal together when they hardly knew each other.

He turned suddenly. 'Is this bothering you?'

It was bothering her that she was almost enjoying herself. Whose stupid idea had this been anyway? 'Not at all,' she said. 'It gets the meal on the table quicker.'

He smiled and Zoe felt her heart beating faster. *Stop it,* she told herself. *Remember Neil.*

How had this happened? One moment Connor was reluctantly offering to babysit, not wanting a reminder of what life might have been like had things gone to plan four years ago but not seeing that he had any option—and the next he was agreeing to an intimate supper with an attractive woman! He didn't need this sort of complication. Zoe didn't appear to be offering anything more than food, but he was going to have to make it plain that if she was, there was nothing doing. That would hurt. It would hurt her to be rejected, and it would hurt him to be the one turning her down. It would have been very much simpler had he just gone home as soon as she arrived back.

But he hadn't, so he would eat supper with a good grace, make general unthreatening conversation and try not to dwell on the fact that in the normal course of events, he would have found Zoe very alluring indeed.

Connor focused on the generously filled plates. Ham, quartered eggs, sliced new potatoes, pickles and a mound of salad. 'If this is your idea of a small meal, I'd hate to see what you'd lay on for a starving man,' he said.

'You don't have to finish it,' she replied, transferring the plates to the table.

'That would be plain rude.' He picked up the Rioja and

stopped her sweeping away the cork as she wiped down the worktop. 'Whoa. I'll need that to re-cork the wine.'

She stared at him, her hand flying to her mouth.

'What's the matter?'

'Nothing. It's just that Neil never put a cork back in a bottle of wine in his life.'

In an instant, the atmosphere changed. Zoe's colour was high, but she had the air of having meant every word. 'He was an alcoholic,' she said simply, and sat down opposite him to eat.

Connor was dumbfounded. He could deal with statements like that in the surgery during his working day. In the kitchen, when all he was expecting was a salad supper with a colleague, they were rather more difficult.

She stretched across the table and put her hand on his arm. 'It doesn't matter. It's in the past. It seemed like a good opportunity to tell you, that's all. Can we talk about something else, please?'

He poured both of them a glass of wine. 'To be honest, I'm not sure what I should say anyway.' He lifted his Rioja, inhaling the aroma and taking a sip, giving himself time to think.

She drank too. 'This is very nice. I must remember to thank the assistant in the shop.'

Connor recognised the deliberately cheerful style. So be it. Soul-searching over a meal always gave him indigestion anyway. 'It's grand,' he said. 'Not just the wine—the food and the company as well. It makes a change from eating alone.'

The tension went out of her. 'Thank you.' They both knew it wasn't thanks for the compliment.

'So, what was the call tonight?' he asked, applying himself to his plate. 'Any emergencies we need to look out for?'

He'd said it to make casual conversation, but Zoe hesitated. 'Not an emergency,' she said carefully. 'More of a friendly visit. I'd say more, but it's not really my story to tell.'

Connor groaned. 'Another Jo Summers special, in fact.'

She fired up at that. 'Jo is my friend and I love her. It's not her fault that she has the biggest heart in the universe. It's all right—no notes were taken, no drugs prescribed. And, for what it's worth, she was absolutely right. We did need to go.'

Now he knew something else about her. She was loyal, especially to the people she cared about. 'I'm not arguing. This food and this wine are too good to spoil.'

Zoe grinned. 'I agree. Tell me about Buckley and the Peak District instead. What else do I need to know about life up here?'

Astonishing, thought Zoe as she cleared away. Their one glass of wine had lasted all through the meal. Connor had corked the bottle and—after a small argument—put it ready to take back with him. So very different from other meals in her past. And as a bonus, after that initial awkwardness, she'd enjoyed chatting to him. She was no nearer finding out why he was reserved at work and more outgoing at home, but it didn't seem to matter.

'Would you like a coffee?' she asked. 'We could take it onto the patio to drink.'

'I think I would. Yes, please.'

The sun was sinking, casting long shadows over her little lawn. The light had that particular late-evening quality that tinted everything it touched with gold. A magic time of day.

They sat outside, one in each wicker chair. He stirred his coffee thoughtfully, then glanced up and their eyes met. All of a sudden, Zoe had an odd feeling of adventure, as if she were doing something slightly dangerous. How ridiculous. It was simply that they'd finished eating so there was nothing to occupy them. They were thrown fully into each other's company.

'I really love sunset here,' she said.

'Yes. As if the day's cares are being wound up. I've often sat here and thought so.'

But now he couldn't, because she and Jamie were in residence. She bit her lip. 'I feel guilty, robbing you of your view.'

He shrugged. 'I'm sure if I exert myself I can find a west-facing window in my house.'

A small silence fell between them.

'Zoe—'

'Connor—'

He gestured. 'Ladies first.'

She took a deep breath. This had to be said, and it had to be said now. For much the same reason as her telling him about Neil's alcoholism earlier. She didn't want him labouring under any misapprehensions. 'Connor, remember that spark that passed between us when we first met?'

'Very well. You shouted "Ow". It was just static electricity.'

'Just static electricity? Didn't you feel something else passing between us? Something affecting us both?'

He turned his head and looked at her directly. Unflinchingly, she stared back, noticing that his face had gone blank. Impossible to guess what he was thinking. Oh, Lord, had she got this completely wrong? After what seemed an age, he slowly said, 'Yes, I felt it.'

'Well, thank goodness for that,' she said with a nervous laugh. 'Otherwise I'd be *really* embarrassing myself.'

'You could just stop,' he suggested.

Zoe shook her head determinedly. 'That's not my way. What I'm going to say might sound conceited, and forward, and completely jumping the gun, but we need to get it out in the open. I—'

'Zoe, if you're about to make a pass at me, I think you should know that—'

'I'm not!' She stared at him, utterly shocked.

'Then I'm the one who's embarrassed. I'd better go.'

'I was going to warn *you* off making a pass at *me*!'

They stared at each other in the roseate light. This time the silence was horrible.

'You can't blame me for thinking you might,' burst out Zoe.

'We're becoming friends, you've babysat my son, we've shared a meal. I just didn't want you to think it might lead somewhere.' But looking at him now, impersonal and distant, she didn't see how she could have imagined any such thing.

'I *know* it won't lead anywhere for me,' he said quietly. 'I'm curious, though. Why won't it on your part?'

Zoe lifted her coffee mug to her lips, let the warmth dispel the solid embarrassment inside her. 'I was in love with Neil when I married him. He was very charismatic, a real live wire. When I was with him it was like being on a permanent holiday. I realise now that my feelings were partly reaction from having looked after Mum for so long and being free at last. I'm not excusing, I'm not complaining, I'm just saying that we were genuinely in love. We were still in love when we had Jamie. And then…then I realised that Neil couldn't slow down. He didn't know how to and he didn't want to. He drank far too much, but wouldn't admit that he had a problem. He was drunk when he crashed the car.'

Connor's hand brushed hers. 'I'm sorry. But all men aren't like that, you know.'

She looked at him, dry-eyed. 'He was bringing Jamie home from a birthday party. Jamie had nightmares for ages. Sometimes he still does.'

'Oh, no.' The words were an appalled whisper.

'Neil promised he'd never drink when Jamie was around. He lied. I'm never going to compromise my son's safety again, Connor. Never, ever. And that means I doubt I'll ever trust a man not to let me—or Jamie—down again.'

They finished their coffee as the sun finally melted along the horizon. Connor stood up and just touched Zoe's cheek for a moment. 'Don't brood tonight,' he said. 'Think about whatever good you did today instead.'

She closed her eyes for a moment and, unbidden, the images of two men came into her mind. Neil and Connor;

she thought of them side by side. Two totally different men. When first she had known him, Neil had swept her off her feet. He was outgoing, noisy, the life and soul of every party; she had loved every minute of being with him in those early days. Connor was quieter, but just as charismatic in his way. She remembered a phrase once used by a consultant she had worked for. Connor was better grounded than Neil.

The memory of what Neil had been at the end came back; he had changed so much. Perhaps Connor could change too. It saddened her, but stiffened her resolution.

She walked with him to the gate. The night sky was beautiful, hints of green in the blue. That was something she had never seen in London. 'There's a star,' she said, pointing. 'Just one, bright in the sky.'

He looked up. 'It's called the Evening Star, but really it's the planet Venus, not a star at all.'

Venus. The goddess of love. Well, she was out of luck tonight. She might have two single people—already attracted— in her sights, but there would be no romantic outcome.

*Wait a minute!* Zoe's mind back-tracked. 'How do you know it won't lead anywhere?'

'I beg your pardon?'

'You said you knew that whatever *isn't* between us wouldn't lead anywhere. What makes you so sure?'

Connor's voice was remote. 'Because I got burned once as well—very badly. It makes you fear the fire. And I suspect neither of us is interested in casual affairs. I'm certainly not.'

Zoe shuddered. 'Nor me. I don't see how an affair *can* be casual.'

'So—just friends then.'

'Just friends.'

They touched hands by mistake, both reaching for the gate. 'See?' said Connor. 'No spark.'

Warmth burned to the very core of her. A bespoke lightning conductor couldn't have provided a better channel.

'No spark,' she agreed, knowing that it was as far from the truth as it was possible to get.

# CHAPTER FIVE

'YOU'LL like Baby Clinic,' Jo had said confidently in the staff lounge. 'It's fun.'

'Assuming your definition of fun includes temporary deafness and finding toys in every plant pot for the next week,' murmured Connor as he helped himself to coffee.

One of the younger female doctors dropped her cup with a muffled exclamation. Zoe concluded that Connor wasn't famed for making jokes at work.

'It is fun,' insisted Jo. 'All mothers enjoy exchanging horror stories about how dreadful their latest arrivals are. And it's much better for new mums to have their post-natal check-ups here where they can feel part of a group rather than at home where they'll brood about being isolated.'

Looking around the lively group—many of the parents had brought their older children, who were running around the waiting room, scattering the toys all over the floor—Zoe had to give her friend credit. 'It would be difficult to feel isolated in this lot,' she said to the district nurse attached to the practice.

'That's the idea! Right, I'll weigh the babies, you check over the new mothers, and Dr Maitland is the duty doctor if either of us have problems.'

Zoe thoroughly enjoyed her morning. Being an exmidwife, Jo had firm views on the amount of work that could be accomplished safely and happily in the allocated time, so there was no mad rush of patients. Zoe managed a sociable word with most of the women she met. But more than the sense of a job well done was a feeling of belonging. Her questions to the mums weren't a one-way street. There was friendly curiosity from them too, personal questions. Zoe realised that if she was to become part of the community she had to give them something of herself. That was fine by her—with reservations.

A couple of times she buzzed Connor for advice, and couldn't help tingling when she talked to him. Had they really said all that last night? Had she really been so blushingly frank? He had left quite quickly after they had come to their agreement—if agreement it was. He hadn't *seemed* embarrassed in the staff room first thing, but she was coming to realise that he was a master at concealing his feelings.

What did astonish her was when a pale young woman was ushered into the clinic by a beaming Jo. 'Barbara Reagan has just signed back on with us,' said her friend, not quite keeping the satisfaction out of her voice. 'I'll get her notes transferred across, but can you just check her over in the meantime?'

'I did what you suggested,' said Barbara, her voice surprisingly determined. 'When Roy came in I told him that I wanted to re-register at the Centre. We had an argument; he got angry and said he was going back to the pub. I told him I'd been thinking of our trip to Filey and that I needed to remember happier days. He was really taken aback. I don't think he realised I was properly unhappy. Then he saw I wasn't crying, that I was calm and...well, we had a bit of a talk, and he agreed.'

'That's brilliant! I'd like you and the little girls to have a full check-up, if that's all right? Which doctor did you used to see?'

'Whoever was handy. But I liked Dr Maitland. When I was first pregnant and a bit doubtful about things, he told me how lucky I was to be having a baby and that made me feel a lot better.'

'That was nice of him.' Zoe tucked the snippet into the store of things she was learning about Connor. 'He's the duty doctor this morning. Would you like to see him now instead of making a regular appointment?'

'That would be great. It's a bit of a struggle getting out with both the kids.'

'Right. Pop back out to the waiting room and catch up with the other mums—I'll find out when Dr Maitland is free.' Pausing only to check with Jo that she didn't mind Zoe telling Connor about visiting Barbara last night, she sped upstairs to his consulting room.

Connor listened impassively, shutting off all signs of emotion as she told him about Barbara, her children and her husband. She had no idea whether he felt sympathy or irritation, or what he thought of her part in the story. It was very off-putting. She hoped he was more approachable with his patients.

When she had finished he looked at her steadily. 'You do know that severe cases of baby blues can lead to suicide?'

'I'd be a pretty poor midwife not to.'

'And that if there is even the smallest suggestion of that, our duty is to inform the authorities?'

Zoe felt herself growing angry. 'Yes, I know. Yes, of course I would inform them, no matter how accidentally I came to be there. In my *professional* opinion, Dr Maitland, what Barbara Reagan is suffering from is having two babies a year apart and an unsympathetic husband.'

'I had to ask, Zoe.'

For some reason this made her even crosser. 'No, you didn't. You could have trusted my judgement, seen Barbara and her little girls and then had a case consultation afterwards.'

He remained cool. 'It wasn't personal. I would have asked any of my colleagues the same question.'

'Then you should have more faith in us. Will you come down and see Barbara now?' She was being as crisp as he was. That wasn't like her. She moved to the door, not asking herself why she should be so hurt.

For the rest of the day, Connor couldn't shake off the feeling that Zoe was disappointed in him. But that was crazy. He was a fully qualified doctor; he had to look out for the interests of the practice and he'd only known Zoe a few days. She'd been dead right about Barbara Reagan, though. Was he going to have to apologise? With the thought came a knock on his kitchen door.

Jamie stood on the path, smiling confidently at him. 'Hello, Uncle Connor. Can I play on your swings, please? Mummy says I must ask.'

And there was Zoe, standing a little way behind him, her expression a study in mingled pride and awkwardness.

'Of course you can,' said Connor. He kept a straight face. 'It was very polite of you to enquire this first time but, from now on, you can use the play dell whenever you like.'

'Told you,' yelled Jamie to his mother, and tore off down the path.

Connor fell into step with Zoe as she followed her son. She'd changed into a summer dress of pale lemon cotton. 'You look nice and cool,' he said. 'That suits you.'

There was just the tiniest pause before she replied. 'Thank you. And thank you for giving Jamie the run of the play area. We'll only be an hour. He just needs to let off steam a bit.'

He didn't like hearing the reservation in her voice. To his surprise, he realised that, whilst he could brush off other people's niggles with him, he wanted to make things right with her. 'Stay as long as you like,' he said gruffly. 'It was lovely seeing him enjoy himself in my garden yesterday.'

She gave a small smile, unbending a little. 'You may regret

that. I don't know where he gets his energy from—he's always up at dawn, raring to go. I suppose he must be really good at school, bottling it all up until he can get home again. If ever we get to be a nuisance, just say. If you want to be quiet or if you're entertaining…'

'I don't do entertaining.'

She turned a frowning face to him. 'Why not?'

Zoe Hilton: asker of hard questions. 'I spent a year being prodded, poked, tested and interrogated. I was a case, not a person. I certainly wasn't a person with rights. So I don't want anyone invading my space again.' Even to his own ears, his voice sounded harsh. He'd blown it. Zoe would now grab her son's hand and exit the garden with all speed.

Instead, she sighed. 'You are one contrary man, Connor Maitland.'

She hadn't run off. Connor could hardly believe it. 'Wanting privacy is contrary?'

'No. Shutting everyone out at work—and opening up to me at home is contrary.'

He shrugged. 'I'm on my own ground here. Maybe that makes the difference.'

She considered him with those wide, thoughtful eyes. 'Why isn't the Medical Centre your own ground? You've spent nine years training for it. You laid down the law fast enough this morning. You walked through that Theatre as if you owned it on my first day here. I don't understand.'

Connor felt as if his mind had suddenly been laid bare. With one statement she'd pinpointed his innermost dilemma, and it felt awful. 'Because…because…' His chest hurt. He could hear his breath tearing. What was she wrenching from him? He looked away, fixed his eyes on the hills beyond his garden. 'Because I remember how things used to be,' he said roughly. 'Because GP work has endless threads, whereas surgery is clean and clear-cut and I was very good at it.'

'You're a good doctor. Everybody says so.'

'But I'm not the best,' he ground out, still keeping his eyes fixed on the tree line, the thin zigzag path leading to the summit. He'd rather be pounding up that track right now than answering these questions. 'And other things are wrong and I can't fix them.'

'For instance?'

'For instance, in the hospital I saw a patient of mine who isn't getting better. Percy Spenloe is eighty-six. I recommended him for the heart bypass operation. I pulled strings to get him on the fast track. I'm damn sure if I'd done the op he'd have been home by now. But he's not thriving! I'm irritating the hell out of the consultant by suggesting tests when he's done them all already and they've come back negative. I feel so frustrated!'

'Well, I think that's reasonable,' said Zoe. 'It's part of human nature to think we're better than the next person when it comes to our own speciality.' Her brow wrinkled. 'Spenloe… It's an unusual name. Any relation to Karen Spenloe? Twenty-five weeks pregnant with her fourth child—her middle girl is in Jamie's class—I saw her earlier in the week.'

'Yes, she's one of my patients. Percy's granddaughter-in-law. She told me all her babies have popped out like shelling peas and she wanted a home birth for this one, despite the fact that there's no room in that house to swing a kettle, let alone clear a dedicated birth space. How she and her husband ever find the privacy to procreate is a complete mystery to me. Every time I went to visit Percy I was tripping over children, toys or puppies at every step.'

She grinned, but there was still that serious wrinkle across her forehead. Connor found himself fascinated by it. 'That's interesting. When she saw me, Karen was adamant that she only wants to be in the maternity unit for the minimum time to have her next baby. "In, give birth, quick cuppa and home again," was how she put it. Said she'd worry what the family was getting up to without her, otherwise. And Percy lives with them?'

'Everyone lives with them! Karen and her husband, the kids, a couple of cousins, her mother, his father and Grandpa Percy too. I think there's even a stray aunt tucked into the broom cupboard.'

Zoe chuckled. 'I'll bet that makes visiting time at the hospital interesting.'

Connor groaned. 'Tell me about it. I had my ear bent by the ward sister yesterday. The Spenloes take over the place, sitting on the unused beds, bringing Percy unsuitable things to eat, turning the patients' TVs on for them, wrecking the radio headsets. The only reason they don't get thrown out is that Percy brightens up when they're there.' He slammed his fist into his palm. 'There has to be something we've all missed. I'll get them to do the tests again, no matter how unpopular it makes me. If only I was on the spot all the time! I'm sure I'd…'

To his astonishment, Zoe put her finger on his lips. 'You know your trouble? You're thinking like a surgeon. That worked to get Percy in there—you have the knowledge and the clout that saved his life. But in order to *keep* his life, you need to think like a GP.'

He stared at her. Think like a GP? What did she mean? But…but he did dimly see. A GP had access to the patient's life. A GP looked at the whole person, not just the narrow ramifications of the operation in question.

Zoe's eyes were bright. Her half-smile told him that he knew the answer really; all he had to do was fetch it forth from his brain. He had to let go of his anger and *think*.

'Oh, for goodness' sake,' he said softly, every muscle still. 'Are you telling me Percy is homesick?'

The smile became full and beaming. 'Me? I've never even met him. You're his doctor.'

Connor looked at his watch, already fumbling his mobile out of his pocket and flipping it open. 'Just time. The consultant will still be there. I'll spring Percy for the weekend and he can go back on Monday or Tuesday for a check-up.' He dropped a distracted kiss on her hair. 'Thanks, Zoe, I owe you one.'

Zoe didn't see Connor again all weekend. This, she told herself, was a Very Good Thing. It gave her time to organise that thank you kiss into the back of her mind where it belonged. It would have been nice to forget it completely, but she couldn't quite manage that. The soft press of his lips against her hair, allied to the joy at potentially solving his problem and the speed with which he wanted to put that solution into action were all bound together into a jubilant memory. He'd been so *different* from the way he was in the surgery. She'd had a tiny flash that this was how he was supposed to be. She felt she was getting to know him. How could she want to forget that?

Saturday was spent with Jo and her family, which was lovely. The only awkward moment was when Jamie talked about 'Uncle Connor's' playground.

'Uncle Connor?' said Jo, eyebrows lifting.

'He calls you and Sam Auntie and Uncle, doesn't he?'

'Absolutely. Perfectly understandable. I'm glad you're all getting on.'

Jo looked so bland that Zoe refused to gratify her by asking anything else about Connor. Instead, she turned the conversation to various old friends, and then listened to Jo's grand plans for the Medical Centre.

In private, however, she thought about him quite a lot. Why, for instance, did he not have a partner and children of his own? She'd read up all she could find on Lyme disease but it was irritatingly patchy. There were possible links to infertility, a small percentage of relapses, but the vast majority of sufferers recovered and went on to live normal lives. So what was the problem? Zoe just wanted to understand.

On Sunday she and Jamie used the play area both before and after lunch, but there was no sign of life from the big house. Connor was evidently out for the day.

On Monday morning Karen Spenloe was holding court by the school gate, full of praise for marvellous Dr Maitland. 'He saw right away that Grandpa Percy would be better off at home with his own telly and porridge and chips if he felt like it and his mates coming in for a game of cards and all that. And he came to see him yesterday—on a Sunday—just to check on him.'

There were murmurs of approval from the other parents. Zoe tried to slip around the group to drop off Jamie, but Karen spotted her. 'And he said it might be all right, me having the baby at home, if you say yes as well.'

'Really?' said Zoe, affecting surprise. 'Well, he's changed his mind since we had our case conference about you on Friday. Because *then* we both agreed that, as comfortable as home births are, we knew you'd much rather the baby was born safe and sound in Sheffield maternity unit with the most up-to-date medical care possible available at a moment's notice.'

Karen was impressed at being the subject of a case conference. 'Oh, well,' she said, 'he didn't say all that really— but if you don't ask, you don't get, do you?'

And now it was late afternoon and Zoe was once more sitting on the curved bench around Connor's play area, answering emails from friends on her laptop while Jamie played. The weather couldn't stay this pleasant for ever—but, even if it changed to driving rain for a week, she still thought she'd enjoy life more here with nothing to do but huddle inside than she would being back in buzzing, busy London. She was telling all her disbelieving friends so when Jamie called, 'Look at me, Mummy!'

Zoe looked up and set her laptop aside immediately. Jamie had jumped off the swing and started scrambling up the climbing frame. Zoe didn't like the frame. In her view, it was far too high for a five-year-old. He might fall and… She shuddered at the thought. She knew there would be a soft landing; the gardener had spread fresh bark there, but she still went to stand underneath and held her arms up to him when he called that he was going to crawl along the top of the frame.

'I'm all right,' he shouted when he saw her. 'Don't need you; I can do it.'

'You might fall, Jamie.'

Now he was getting annoyed with her. 'Not going to fall. Go away.'

'He's all right,' a calm voice behind her said. 'Little boys have to climb.'

She turned. She hadn't heard Connor approach. 'Little girls have to climb too. I tried to when I was his age but I wasn't allowed.'

'Why not? Because it wasn't the done thing? Or because your parents were protective?'

'I don't know. It doesn't matter now. But I worry about Jamie. I can't help it.'

Connor put his hands on her arms, gently urging her backwards, away from the climbing frame. The thrill of his touch was there again, warring with umbrage that he was taking charge.

'Look, Uncle Connor! I'm swinging.' Jamie was hanging by his hands, smiling.

Instinctively, Zoe lunged forward. Connor's hold tightened. 'He'll be all right. Leave him.' He held her arms just a little too long. Part of her—shockingly—wanted to lean back and let him take over. She shook him off, appalled. No way did Connor Maitland know better than her what was right for her son.

'Look, Mummy, I'm swinging again.'

This time she managed not to move to be nearer him.

Instead, she turned to look at Connor. She had noticed that, like her, he always changed when he got home. Today being warm, he was in light chinos and a white T-shirt. In the Medical Centre he always looked professional, like a doctor. When dressed casually, his masculinity was more obvious. Then she thought of herself in shorts and a loose shirt. Nothing like a midwife.

Connor's usually well-controlled expression was in abeyance as she spun round. Just for a moment, she saw longing in his face. Longing for her? His eyes were on her. She didn't know, but the thought dried her mouth.

He changed the subject. 'How was your weekend? Did you get a chance to show Jamie the countryside?' he asked.

'No. We went to Jo's and then finished settling in. I'm looking forward to a bit of exploration once we've got our bearings. It's a bit terrifying, though—all this open space. Do you know the area well?'

'Pretty well. I used to climb here quite a bit, long before I moved. I still walk now and again. Not so much as I did.'

She thought she detected a touch of sadness in his voice. 'Because you're not as fit as you were?'

'Something like that.'

Sometimes, Zoe found herself just saying things without thinking them through, without considering the consequences. 'I was thinking of taking Jamie out for the day on Saturday. Pack sandwiches and go for a walk. I don't suppose you'd like to come with us? Show us a nice route?'

She saw the surprise in his eyes and flinched. 'Sorry, I shouldn't have said that. The last thing you must want is to go out with someone you hardly know and a young boy while you're…'

'I've not been out walking with anyone for months.' His voice became challenging. 'Did you ask me because you wanted to walk with me? Or because you think it would be good for me?'

'Neither.' Now Zoe was cross with herself. 'I'm trying to do this whole countryside thing properly, trying to make this a complete change of life. But I'm not sure I really know what I'm doing and I'd like Jamie and me to start off walking with someone I trust.' She paused and then added honestly, 'But I suppose I do think a bit more human contact wouldn't kill you.'

He looked at her with mild exasperation. 'You do realise you've just made it impossible for me to refuse? Okay, Saturday. The weather forecast is set fair. There are several trails for novices and…if you like, I could introduce Jamie to real climbing.'

'Real climbing! He's only five!'

'The perfect age for him to start learning properly. He'll absorb the discipline; you'll stop worrying. He needs it, Zoe, and he needs it now. Look at him. Trying to imitate man's ape ancestors.'

Jamie had his hands on the overhead bars, his feet on the ladder at the end of the frame. He was almost horizontal.

'Jamie!' Zoe gave a little squawk of fear. She didn't move forward because Connor's hand was straight away on her arm and even though his grip was light she knew she mustn't break it for fear of distracting Jamie.

'You could try climbing yourself,' he suggested. 'There's a sport for beginners called bouldering. You'd have a rope round you so you couldn't fall. If you ask me, though, part of your fear for Jamie is *because* you've never been allowed to fall yourself.'

'You mean you'll show me how to make mistakes?'

'It's an odd way of putting it, but yes.'

This was something she had never thought of, never expected. She liked the thought of a ramble in the countryside, but she wasn't sure she wanted to try climbing. It was something different, but potentially useful.

'It would be good for both of you,' he said. 'It's the sort of thing you ought to be familiar with if you're going to be living in Buckley for any length of time.'

The sort of thing a nice chap would do with his wife and his son, but which Neil wouldn't have done because he couldn't be bothered, because there would always have been something more amusing to take preference.

'Thank you; we'd like to come climbing with you,' she said. 'And now—if it doesn't go against your principles— could you *please* lift Jamie down from your scary frame?'

He laughed, opened his arms to Jamie, and her son happily let go of the bars and slithered into them.

Zoe was delighted to see Barbara Reagan at Baby Clinic again. She was less delighted that Barbara's husband Roy had accompanied her. He lounged at the side of the room, effectively stopping her joining in with the other mums' conversation as she had last week. Zoe watched as the district nurse called Barbara over to have the baby weighed. Roy went too, answering every time Barbara was asked a question, monopolising the conversation. As they returned to their seats he made a couple of chauvinistic remarks to another dad who was there with his wife.

Zoe rang Connor. 'Have you finished your list yet? Can you pop into Baby Clinic?'

'I have finished, but I'm not duty doctor today.'

'I don't need a doctor. I need a distraction. Barbara Reagan's wretched husband is here in macho guard dog mode. He's not letting her say a word for herself. Could you draw him off?'

Connor's voice turned austere. 'No. He's not one of our patients. It would be horrendously unprofessional.'

Zoe ground her teeth. 'But Barbara *is* one of our patients and she needs our help and support. I'm not asking you to talk to Roy as a doctor. Pretend you're waiting for me and just filling in the time. I want to see Barbara by herself to find out how things are going.'

'Why don't I see her and you do the distracting?'

'Because the man's a Neanderthal! He doesn't talk to women; he wipes his feet on them!'

Zoe heard Connor give an irritable sigh. 'All right. If I get sued for malpractice, you can pay the fine.'

Connor stalked into the baby clinic area feeling distinctly ruffled. He saw Barbara and her husband at once. Roy was good-looking, cocksure, lounging at his ease but with his eyes darting everywhere. Connor made a point of spotting Zoe laughing with one of the new mums on the far side of the room, then he glanced at the clock on the wall, checked his own watch and sat down next to Roy as if waiting.

Barbara's eyes flicked quickly sideways. She got up to untangle her older child's jumper just as Zoe walked across.

'I'll see you now, Barbara,' she said. And, to Connor, 'Ten minutes, promise.'

Connor looked at Roy. 'Ha, believe that and you'll believe anything. Women!'

Roy had started to his feet but he turned back at that. By the time he'd said, 'Too right!' the women had disappeared down the consulting room corridor. He subsided, looking angry. 'I wanted to talk to her,' he muttered. 'Filling Bar's head with rubbish. Why should my wife need help in the house, eh? Why should she need to go out to toddler clubs?'

Connor shrugged. 'Doesn't seem unreasonable to me. You see your mates every day, don't you? Women need that sort of support network too.'

Roy looked round the room with a sneer. 'Chattering like magpies.'

'It makes them happy. Who knows how many things they've solved that were bugging them this morning.'

'I suppose Bar *has* been brighter this week,' Roy said grudgingly. 'Drives me nuts when she's weepy all the time. That's half the reason I go to the pub. Then I say things I don't mean and she starts wailing again and the kids start up too and...'

'There you go, then. Having help in the house will make her less tired as well.'

'Mum never had help. Dad wouldn't have allowed it.'

'Yeah, but you're not your dad, are you?' Connor swung the bag he was carrying, wondering how much longer Zoe was going to be. He couldn't string this conversation out for much longer without Roy realising he had a vested interest.

'Are those climbing boots?' said Roy in a different tone.

'Yes, they're ones my nephew has outgrown. I'm hoping they'll fit the midwife's little boy. I promised to start him bouldering this weekend.'

'Climbing, eh? I used to do a bit of that.' Roy was definitely more alert now.

'Grand pastime, isn't it. Out there matching yourself against the slopes. Why did you stop?'

'Oh, you know. Got a job. No time. Mates started taking the mickey.'

'You'd have the last laugh if you got yourself onto a rescue team. You'd be a hero. Why not take it up again? Got a favourite route?'

Connor rather enjoyed the look on Zoe's face when she returned with a very much happier Barbara to find Roy talking animatedly about gullies and buttresses.

'What did you say?' she murmured as Roy helped his wife gather up kids and possessions and pushed the pram out of the surgery without making any further trouble.

'Reminded him of the good things in life. And all without disturbing any medical ethics.'

Despite her reservations, Zoe was enjoying herself. They were walking through woodland, up a rough track towards a line of rocks. Jamie was riding on Connor's back, perched on top of his rucksack. As promised, the weather was good—the sun warm but with a cooling breeze and the air like champagne.

She felt a sense of adventure, of starting something new. And—she admitted it privately—there was the pleasure of being with Connor. He looked every inch the climber, dressed in once expensive but now well-worn kit. He had a coiled red rope over his shoulder. He always seemed a confident man, but today he seemed confident in a different way. Confident and content.

He slowed down and Zoe looked doubtfully at the great outcrop of millstone grit that stretched in front of them. 'You're not going to make us climb that, are you?'

He laughed. 'No, but I bet it won't be long before you want to try. We're going to climb that little slab.'

Zoe looked where he pointed. 'Connor, that's the height of my house!'

He had opened the rucksack, took out of it a jumble of straps and tapes. 'I've got one of these for both of you. Jamie, this is a safety harness. It's to keep you safe when you climb.'

Jamie was intrigued. 'Can I wear it on the climbing frame?'

'I wish,' muttered Zoe. She watched as Connor swiftly connected a series of straps round Jamie's little body. And then, very excitingly as far as her son was concerned, fastened a small helmet on his head.

'I used these for my nephews and nieces,' he said. 'Before…' His voice trailed away.

'Before what?' She knew she had to ask.

'I couldn't climb, I couldn't even walk to begin with, while I was ill.' He couldn't disguise the pain in his voice.

She put her hand fleetingly over his. 'These things happen. You're better now.'

He sighed. 'Yes.'

She pretended to sound anxious. 'At least, I hope you're better, because if we get into difficulties you're going to have to rescue us.'

He gave a lopsided smile. 'I've still got a residual stiffness in my knee joints, but for the sort of climbing we're going to do today I'm recovered enough. Your turn. Step into these two loops.'

There were buckles to fasten, straps to pass round her waist and over her shoulders. She would never have worked it out on her own so he did it for her and she tried to ignore the ripples of pleasure as his arms passed round her waist, his fingers accidentally brushed across her breasts. 'You look like a real climber,' he said encouragingly. 'You can try first and Jamie can watch and then he won't be worried when we try him on something smaller.'

He unwrapped the red rope, tied a loop in one end and fastened it to a metal ring in the front of her harness; he called it a carabiner. Then he tied the other end to the harness round his own waist. They were tied together. And immediately she felt safe.

'We're going to climb this first,' he said and led her to a sloping bit of grey rock with the cliff rearing above it.

'Right to the top?' she quavered.

'No. Just up the sloping bit, the slab. But after a few visits you will want to climb to the top. And there's a smaller boulder round the corner just right for Jamie.'

It struck her that he was talking about future trips with her. She hadn't expected this when they arranged to come out together just for one day. But, she had to admit, she liked the idea. This was the kind of thing that friends did together.

*Friends?* A little voice echoed in her mind. *And can you keep it that way?*

Connor walked to the foot of the slab, put his hands on it and then climbed upwards. It looked so easy! And he looked amazingly graceful! 'Things to remember,' he called down as he climbed. 'One—only move one foot or one hand at a time. Always have three bits of you on the rock, either two hands and a foot, or two feet and a hand. Two—try to keep upright, keep your body away from the rock, don't hug it. This puts all your weight on your feet—which is where you want it.'

Then he was on the top of the slab, seated on a ledge. He did complicated things with the rope, tying it behind him, then pulled up the slack so the rope was taut between them. 'I'm belayed,' he called down, 'which means I'm tied down. Climbers should always be belayed for safety. I can easily take your weight now, so come up and join me.'

She turned, looked at the fascinated Jamie. Then she looked at the rock, Connor perched above her. It was only the height of her house. No great height. Not that she would try to climb up the wall of her house. Even with a ladder.

There were hand holds and foot holds, but what Connor had made look easy was really quite hard. She inched her way upwards, the secure harness giving her confidence. In a couple of places she really had to struggle. 'Stretch your left foot out; there's a crack there you can get some purchase in.' He was right.

She was three-quarters of the way up, nearly there. 'Stop there a minute,' Connor shouted. 'Make yourself comfortable. Now take both hands off the holds and rest them flat against the rock.'

The man was mad! 'Won't I fall?' she called up at him.

'No, you won't. For a start, I've got you tight. Now take your hands off the holds.'

It took great effort of will but she did as he said. And she didn't fall. She was balanced on two feet. Here she was, this far off the ground, only a couple of inches of rock stopping her from falling. It was scary. No, it was more than that; it was exhilarating. 'Now come up the rest of the way,' he called.

She climbed to the top of the slab; he moved along the ledge and made room for her to sit, then he tied her rope to the finger of rock he was tied to. 'I made it,' she said, hardly believing it. 'Connor, that was terrifying, but also completely exhilarating, I loved it! Thank you so much! Gosh, I feel all trembly and excited.'

He seemed as thrilled as she was. 'You did splendidly!' He put his arm round her for a congratulatory hug and made to kiss her on the cheek. Except that she turned her head towards him at the same time, so the kiss landed on her mouth.

Oh, Lord. Oh, good heavens. His mouth was firm and his skin was warm, with a faint citrus tang from his aftershave. Zoe's heart gave one enormous thump. Her body flooded with heat and she felt all her nerve endings come alive. Her lips were parting before she realised it, certainly before she realised that he was drawing back.

What had she nearly done? What had *they* nearly done? 'I'm sorry,' he said, 'I didn't mean to…' but his eyes were riveted on her mouth and she knew he'd been as affected by the near-embrace as she had.

She tried to conquer her breathlessness. 'Please…you needn't apologise for kissing me,' she said. 'I liked it. It was exactly the right way to end my first climb.'

But he didn't seem to be listening to her. He'd bent his head, was rummaging in his backpack. Zoe noticed beads of sweat on his forehead. He fished out a handkerchief and blotted them, took a swig from his water bottle before passing it to her.

'Mummy, Mummy, my turn now!' There was a little form below them, waving.

Connor cleared his throat. 'Better get down. We have another customer. No need to climb back; there's an easy scramble down just to your right. You go first; I'll keep the rope on you till you're down.'

It was an easy scramble and, although it should have occupied her mind, it didn't. Instead, she was fixing every fluttering micro-second of that gentle kiss into her memory. Whether he'd meant it or not, it had felt very, very special. It was probably a good thing that he was now pretending it had never happened.

It was Jamie's turn next. Connor led them to a boulder a little further on with an easier, much less steep climb of about twelve feet. He treated Jamie exactly as he had treated her. Hugely excited, Jamie scampered up the climb. Then he insisted on doing it again. And again.

'Different this time,' Connor said. 'Mummy's going to belay you.'

She's going to do what? Zoe wondered. But Connor showed her how to fasten herself to the rock behind, how to pass the rope under one arm and over the opposite shoulder, how to keep the rope taut. And she brought up her son. 'Top-roped' him, Connor said. It was a totally different kind of excitement, something she had never experienced before. And she loved it.

'I like climbing,' said Jamie. 'Can we do another one?'

But Connor obviously knew how easy it was to overtire children. 'Time for lunch,' he said. 'And then we'd better get back. I've got some work I should be doing this afternoon.'

He avoided Zoe's eyes. Zoe suspected the 'work' was an excuse so he could forget the kiss and the fact that they'd all got closer than he was comfortable with today. She opened her rucksack and took out orange juice and flask and food. She'd insisted that if Connor was doing the driving and organising the climbing, then she would prepare a picnic. 'Just so long as you don't think that it's obviously woman's work to do the food,' she had told him. 'Comes the time, I'll expect you to make the sandwiches.'

But it didn't look as though there would be another time now. She could feel him distancing himself. That ought to suit her—she didn't want relationship complications any more than he did—but she still wanted him to know just what he'd done for her today.

'I feel different,' she said. 'I don't know what it is but I feel I've taken some kind of step. I've climbed something and I've had the confidence to let Jamie climb. I feel better for it.'

'Good. That was the idea.'

They ate and drank for a few minutes in silence. Zoe was surprised at how hungry she and Jamie were.

'That's a high cliff, Uncle Connor,' said Jamie. 'Could you climb it?' He pointed to the vast and vertical face behind the boulder they had just climbed on.

Connor looked at it, his eyes bleak. 'Oh, yes,' he said. 'I already have.' Then he added in an odd voice, 'In a different life.'

Zoe looked at his face in alarm. He seemed to have forgotten they were there. He stood, flexing his fingers reflectively, then walked over to the boulder Jamie had climbed and ran up it. He didn't even need to use his hands. Then, to Zoe's horror, he started to climb further. 'Connor,' she called, her voice suddenly sharp, 'what are you doing? Come back down, you're being silly.'

But he paid no attention, and she didn't dare shout again in case she disturbed him.

This wasn't an easy slab like the one she had climbed; this face was almost vertical. He climbed upwards, his movements still fluid, graceful, but he was moving much more slowly. Zoe was fearful; she wanted to look away, but daren't. It was as if the sheer intensity of her gaze would help him. He neared the top. It was completely vertical and there were short stretches where she was sure there were no holds at all, where no one could possibly climb. But somehow he did. And finally he hauled himself over the edge, stood and waved. Jamie waved back enthusiastically. 'Are you going to do that, Mummy?'

'No.' Zoe's fear for Connor's safety had been replaced by a deep anger.

Connor disappeared, reappearing a few minutes later having scrambled down a gully. She looked at him, scared to her bones and icy from his unwitting betrayal. 'That was thoughtless and selfish. What did you think you were doing?' she asked, trying to keep the anger in her voice down. 'And what was that you said about always being belayed? Connor, I was terrified. Did you stop to ask yourself what would we have done if you had fallen? Were you hoping to impress me? There was no need; I was impressed already. Now I think you're foolhardy and I remember someone else who was like that and I…' She stopped, turning her head away and trying to control her shuddering breathing.

He reached for her but she jerked away.

The faint triumph in his bearing withered. 'I didn't think. I'm sorry, Zoe, really I am. I wasn't trying to impress you. It was just that I used to run up faces like that easily and I'd not done any serious climbing for so long that I thought I'd never get up the confidence to do them again. But today my confidence came back. I wanted to take a step—just like you said you did. I wanted to stretch myself, prove that the me I remember is still there.'

There was genuine remorse in his face and in his voice. But Zoe had seen remorse before, and suddenly she couldn't bear it that all the men she'd ever cared about were the same. Did what they wanted first, apologised later. Then did it all over again. For a while today, she'd very nearly allowed herself to dream. But she wouldn't repeat that mistake; her heart wasn't strong enough to withstand being hurt again. 'Sorry,' she said. 'I overreacted.' She reached for the Thermos of coffee, her hand shaking.

Connor noticed. He covered her hand and stroked her wrist with his thumb. 'Zoe, I wouldn't upset you for anything. But sometimes the memories of how things used to be are so strong that I…'

She believed him, but somehow that didn't help at all. To push the thoughts away, she opened a foil-covered package. 'Have another sandwich,' she said. 'You need one after all that exertion.'

They were silent for a moment or two. 'Have I blown the chance of any future outings?'

There was only one possible sane answer to that. She should seize on it firmly and quickly and save herself any heartache right now. But…

Zoe rubbed her forehead. 'No, of course you haven't blown the chance. Just remember that I have memories too, Connor. And they aren't pleasant.'

# CHAPTER SIX

CONNOR had shut down his consulting room computer and was preparing to go home when his mobile rang.

'Connor?' It was Zoe, and she sounded rattled.

'Yes, what's up?' As always, just the sound of her voice made his body sit up and take notice. He'd been carefully staying out of her way since the weekend, trying to get her out of his system. For half a moment, that tantalising accidental kiss had made him feel vibrantly alive—then he'd had a dizzy, light-headed, spots-before-the-eyes panic attack, just as he'd had in the bad days of his illness. He remembered Mick saying at the time that he must force himself to relax through them, that tensing up would make his condition worse. He *had* relaxed on Saturday; he had pulled himself together almost immediately, and by distancing himself from Zoe he'd got through the rest of the day to the extent of pulling that stupid stunt with the cliff because he'd been so pleased with himself. Now he concentrated on what she was saying.

'Oh, thank goodness. I'm stuck in traffic in Sheffield and I can't get through to Jo.'

He felt a ludicrous disappointment that it wasn't him she wanted. 'The phone system here has died, that's why. You wouldn't believe how peaceful it's been today. Apart from Jo yelling at BT on her mobile to get an engineer here pronto, which is probably the reason you can't reach her now. Good confinement?'

'No, the baby decided to take a nap halfway through, the mother went into hysterics and we had to use forceps. Connor, can you ask Jo to forget phones for a moment and arrange after-school care for Jamie? They're sending us on a diversion and I haven't the faintest idea where I am or how long I'll be.'

'Yes, of course.' But his conscience pricked him. He'd promised last week that he'd play football with Jamie again and he'd been avoiding him instead. 'Or I could collect Jamie and look after him until you get home,' he said slowly. 'I'm not doing anything else until evening surgery.'

There was a pause when all he could hear was the engine running and distant car horns. 'I'm not going to pretend he wouldn't love that,' she said, equally slowly. 'Are you sure you don't mind?'

'I wouldn't have offered otherwise.'

'Then, thank you.' Her voice sounded a bit strained. 'Connor, don't take this the wrong way, but I'll ring the school to let them know you're collecting him. It's not that I don't trust you—he's all I've got, you see.'

Connor felt his heart twist. 'Tell whoever you like, Zoe.'

It was odd, hovering in the playground waiting for the doors to open. He was aware of the other parents—many of them patients of the Medical Centre—giving him sidelong glances.

Jamie had evidently been briefed. There was a tiny anxious wrinkle the image of Zoe's on his forehead as he scanned the waiting adults—then, when he spotted him, a big beaming smile spread over his face. 'Uncle Connor!' he yelled, and ran across the playground.

Connor opened his arms wide and swung him up. As he did so, an extraordinary truth hit him. This wasn't the same as meeting his nieces and nephews out of school when he'd still lived in Newcastle. Yes, they were family—but Zoe's son had taken hold of his heart.

They turned to go. Connor heard a couple of whispered giggles and saw knowing eyebrows raised on at least one face. He'd have to warn Zoe to expect questions. For now, he just nodded politely, took Jamie's hand in a firm hold and headed for home.

Jamie chattered all the way, and then Connor waited in the coach house kitchen while home clothes were changed into. There was a new picture on the fridge. He smiled as he identified the mended gate, the play area, the long path around Connor's own garden and the lawn where they had played football. He remembered Zoe saying that Jamie only drew what affected him. 'Nice picture,' he said when the little boy thundered downstairs, bursting to go outside and play. 'Who are all the people?'

Jamie gave the fridge a cursory glance. 'You and Mummy.'

'What? All of them?'

'You in your garden. Mummy in our garden. You and Mummy by the swings.' Jamie tugged Connor's hand. 'Can we *play?*'

Connor let himself be pulled towards the gate. Was that why Zoe had sounded strained? Because her son's pictures no longer showed his father in Heaven looking down on him?

They both heard the car at the same time. 'That's Mummy,' said Jamie, and trotted off to meet her.

Over the hedge, Connor saw Zoe shut her car door. She looked tired and drained. He was stunned by a wave of protectiveness. No one should look that exhausted. He wanted to scoop her up, have her nestle into his shoulder and sleep until she'd recovered. But as soon as Jamie called 'Hello, Mummy,' and rattled the gate, she straightened her shoulders and pinned a bright smile on her face. Connor stepped back, not wanting her to realise she'd been observed. It wasn't *right*. She should be looked after at the end of a hard day. She shouldn't have to start all over again, being cheerful and attentive all on her own to a very active little boy. By the time the pair of them had reached the kitchen—Jamie manfully carrying the midwife bag—Connor had the kettle on and her selfish, useless former husband had been damned to the furthest reaches of the afterlife.

'Oh, bless you,' she said. 'I've been gasping for tea for the last ten miles. Did you find the scones? There are some in the blue tin. I must change—I am so hot and sticky.'

He assumed from all this that she expected him to stay on for a bit. Did that mean they were on a better footing again? He was glad, but staying probably wasn't a good idea given the confusion of feelings he was grappling with.

She came down again wearing faded denim shorts and an old yellow T-shirt. Comfort clothes, he diagnosed. 'Thank you for looking after Jamie,' she said, flopping down on the sofa.

'It was no trouble. I enjoyed it.' He sat down in his own shabby, yet comfortable armchair and found himself grinning. He might not be able to see the sunset from here, but he couldn't fault the view of Zoe.

'Uncle Connor taught me to climb on the frame safely,' said Jamie, not looking up from where he was causing a couple of Lego men tied together with string to scale a pile of books.

'Oh, good,' said Zoe faintly.

'I was right under him all the time,' Connor reassured her. All the same, Jamie was a lively kid—however difficult she found it, Zoe *had* to make more of an effort to let him find his own feet. He gave an inward sigh, not seeing how he could get out of this. 'Would you both like to come bouldering again this weekend?'

'He'll never forgive me if I don't say yes.' She gave him a tentative forgive-and-forget smile.

It was the smile that did it. Connor's tongue took off. 'And then another time, I wondered if—can Jamie swim?'

'He can swim very well!' she said indignantly. 'He loves the water.'

'Then perhaps you'd like to try canoeing.'

'Canoeing?'

'There's a club at a reservoir not too far from here. It's something I took up when I couldn't…when I couldn't climb.'

'Well…yes, why not?'

Connor shot a look at Jamie, happily absorbed. He lowered his voice. 'And I should warn you that several parents at school have almost certainly jumped to the wrong conclusion on hearing Jamie yell "Uncle Connor" at me as he raced across the playground.'

'I've coped with worse,' said Zoe wryly.

Another rush of anger. 'What do you mean? Have people been saying things already?'

'Not here. Where we used to live. Neil would sometimes turn up to things the worse for wear. Even my friends would look sideways at me, wondering why I didn't stop him, thinking that maybe it was my fault. And every time I asked if someone would babysit Jamie while I did an extra shift, I could see them feeling sorry for me that I had to work because Neil had spent the housekeeping again.' She gave a brief smile. 'You can see why I'm not in a hurry for another relationship.'

'No, I can understand that.' He held on to his temper and carried on talking, just to fill the silence. 'I think Jamie rushing towards me was mostly relief. He seemed a bit anxious when he first came out.'

Zoe bit her lip. 'He always is. Neil forgot him a couple of times. He *said* a case had come up.'

Connor was even more disgusted. How could anyone forget to collect his own son? And yet she had still loved the man? Still stayed with him? She was loyal, he'd give her that, but all the same, if he didn't get out of here soon he was going to say something he'd regret. 'I'd better go,' he said aloud. 'Evening surgery.'

She got up to see him to the door. 'I tried so hard to make him see sense,' she murmured, almost to herself. 'But he wouldn't admit he needed help. He liked clubbing, he liked drinking. He said it was only social and not to make a silly fuss. He was late picking Jamie up from that birthday party…' She swallowed hard. 'Thank God he was. Because the other kids he was supposed to have given a lift to had gone home by then. I might have had their deaths on my conscience.'

Hell, thought Connor grimly, wasn't good enough for Neil Hilton. 'Zoe—' he began, not knowing how he was going to finish.

She gave him a tired smile. 'I'm sorry. I don't usually whimper like this.'

'Perhaps you should. Get it out of your system.'

She stumbled on a building brick that was lying on the floor. Connor caught her instinctively, held her for a couple of heartbeats. 'I must go,' he said, not wanting to, but not knowing what he did want. 'Will you be all right?'

'I'll be fine. Thanks, Connor. You're a pretty good friend.'

*Friend? Friend?* As Connor strode between the houses, he realised he was perilously close to not settling for *friend* for much longer. It was something he was going to have to fight.

The days slipped by. Zoe was becoming used to her new routine. She looked down with dismay, though, as she stood on the bathroom scales after her morning shower. She had put on five pounds since coming to Buckley! She walked to her bedroom, slipped off the towel and stretched a tape round her waist. No gain there, good. She looked at her naked body, pinched her hips—perhaps they were a bit fuller. She looked at herself again, as critically as possible, and decided that what she had gained was quite in order. But she was not going to put on any more.

She flushed, catching herself thinking that, apart from anything else, she wouldn't fit into Connor's arms if she got any larger. No! She was *not* dwelling on those few moments when she'd felt wonderfully, gloriously safe. Connor didn't want a relationship. She didn't want a relationship. So why were the days when she didn't see him a lot longer than those when she did? And, every time she did see him, there was still that spark. Not a real one any more, but they both knew it was there. And there was always that pleased moment of excitement, that slight increase in her pulse rate that told her the initial attraction hadn't gone away; it was merely being kept under control. She remembered very well the evening on the patio when they had made their agreement. In the sky above had been Venus. Zoe occasionally wondered if the Goddess of Love was now laughing at the pair of them.

'Zoe, are you busy?'

'Hi, Jo. No, just reading up on my patients for this afternoon. Why?'

'We've had an accident case brought in, a woman with a bad cut across her abdomen. She works at the family butchers on the High Street. They've been established there since the year dot and I don't think they've ever quite grasped that we aren't a cottage hospital any more. Anyway, Connor says it's a clean gash and only needs suturing and he's happy to deal with it right now himself rather than send her off to Sheffield, but the practice nurses are working flat out this morning, so I wondered if you could do scrub nurse for him?'

'Yes, of course,' said Zoe immediately. 'As long as it isn't going to tread on anyone's toes. An abdomen cut? How did it happen?'

'Silly woman was wielding one of those giant knives in a

hurry and slipped. Pure accident. You know where to go, don't you? I'll tell Connor to expect you. Thanks, love.'

As soon as Zoe stepped into the scrub room she knew that Connor had metamorphosed into Dominant Surgeon. It was a persona she was entirely familiar with from her hospital days, but it was still weird to see the authority settling around him like a cloak, when only yesterday he'd been chasing her son in and out of the paddling pool with a hose.

'There's a set of greens in the cupboard,' he said now. 'Jo says you've done this before.'

'Lots of times. I was a hospital midwife, Connor. I've assisted consultant gynaecologists in any number of emergencies as well as doing normal scrub nurse duties. I can easily help with a simple suturing.'

On the table a white-faced woman was being attended by a practice nurse. There were bloody bandages on her abdomen and a giving set was transferring plasma to her arm.

'Don't worry, Mrs Prentiss, you're in good hands,' said the nurse. She flashed a smile at Connor and Zoe and hurried back to her clinic.

Connor approached the table. 'Are you quite sure you want me to treat you, Mrs Prentiss? I know you've signed a consent form, but we can still send you to hospital if you'd prefer.'

Mrs Prentiss's voice was hoarse but she knew what she wanted. 'And wait in A&E for hours? You do it, Doctor. You did a lovely job on my neighbour's little girl when she fell and split her lip.'

Connor smiled. Zoe was amused to see that his manner was now a cross between authoritative surgeon and family GP. 'I'll do my best for you. Your husband has been told. I expect he'll be here shortly, but we'll be finished before then. You'll need to stay here the rest of the day—maybe overnight. Will that cause any problems?'

'No. My mother can come round to see to the kids after school.'

'Then we have nothing to worry about. You have two professionals looking after you and you're going to be fine.'

Zoe winced when she saw the size of the injury. It would take some skilful suturing to pull it all together. Someone had already laid out the tray of instruments. There was the local anaesthetic, the cutting and curved needles. There were the absorbable sutures used to stitch the deeper layers to help reduce tension, the non-absorbable sutures for the closure of skin wounds.

Connor nodded at her to start, so she took the bowl of antiseptic and carefully washed the injury.

'I'm going to inject local anaesthetic around the cut, Mrs Prentiss,' said Connor. 'It will sting a little but that will be all. You might feel pressure afterwards but no pain.'

Zoe watched as he injected one per cent lignocaine around the cut, then waited for the anaesthetic to take effect.

'No pain at all? Good, we can start.'

Zoe had sutured herself, particularly after episiotomies, and she had watched consultants suturing, so she could appreciate Connor's skill. He was good and he was fast. And very, very focused. All his attention was on what he was doing, She wasn't his scrub nurse any more; she certainly wasn't his neighbour or tenant. She was simply the pair of hands that gave him whatever he needed. His instructions were crisp but polite. She liked that. They were a working team. She noticed he was taking care to ensure that the scar would be as invisible as possible. A decent-size bikini and Mrs Prentiss would still be able to go to the beach.

It was done in next to no time. Their patient was transferred to a trolley and wheeled to a bed in the small ward next door. The nursing team would be responsible now, though Connor would look in from time to time.

'Beautiful,' said Zoe as they tidied up. 'You are quite some-thing, Dr Maitland.'

He was at the sink, facing away from her. 'I *was* quite something,' he said in a strained voice. 'Zoe, I hate this bit. I hate coming back to the real world.'

'I'd say that was natural. You're the sort of man who won't do anything unless he does it wholeheartedly. It's enormously to your credit that you *can* change from one mindset to another.'

'It's not just the mindset; it's the way of life. It's the whole "big fish in a very important pond" reduced down to—'

'—a perfectly fitting cog in a deeply satisfying team. "Reduced down" nothing! Connor, what you did just now won't ever make the medical journals, but it has saved Mrs Prentiss hours of agony; it's saved her family upheaval and worry—and don't you tell me that any surgeon could have done it because *any surgeon* wasn't here. You were. You've made a difference, Connor. And that's what we're about.'

His back was still turned to her. Had he been listening at all? She desperately wanted to give him a hug, but she knew he wouldn't welcome it. She cast around, aching with sympathy, for something that she *could* do, some way of boosting his self-esteem. 'I suppose it wouldn't help to think of your job in terms of quantity, would it? A top surgeon makes a lifesaving difference to a few patients. A good GP makes hundreds of lives more bearable.'

Still no reply. She gave a silent sigh and finished putting things away.

It was another sunny day. Zoe stepped out of the shower, tucked a towel around herself and opened her bedroom window. She leant her elbows on the sill, breathing in the smell of honeysuckle and lilac. Then straightened up in alarm. Connor, dressed in a baggy grey T-shirt, loose black shorts and flip-flops was loping down the path from his house to hers, looking distinctly irritated.

'What's the matter?' she called, her hand automatically groping for her medical bag.

'Nothing.' The annoyance on his face melted into appreciation, hastily suppressed, as he looked up.

Zoe remembered she was only wearing a towel and pulled it rather tighter.

He turned his face away. 'Is Jamie awake? I remember you said he was an early riser. I've got a video call from my brother in Australia. I told you my mother and father were visiting the family, didn't I? My dear sister has told them all about my new tenants and they're wondering rather pointedly if Jamie would like to see the wallabies in the back yard. You really don't have to say yes.'

'What's a wannabe? I want to see!' Jamie had been playing in the living room and had opened the patio door on seeing Connor outside.

'Yes, all right, but wait a minute,' said Zoe. She hurried down the narrow stairs, still clutching the towel around her.

'Can I see them, Mummy?' Jamie was hopping from one pyjama-clad leg to the other, excited at something out of the ordinary happening before he'd even had breakfast.

'It won't take long,' said Connor, scooping up the small, wriggling body, 'and it'll get them off my back. Sometimes I think they must be starved of news out there. Bless you, Zoe. I'll carry him across while you get some shoes on.'

'And some clothes,' she pointed out. 'Or they'll really be on at you!'

Jamie was already settled in front of the computer screen chattering away when she slipped into the study. Connor's face lightened as he glanced at her T-shirt and shorts. 'Pity,' he murmured, and nodded towards a mug of tea on the coffee table.

'Thank you,' said Zoe, reaching for it.

'Look, Mummy, wanna—no—wallabies!'

'So there are.' To tell the truth, she was far less enthralled by the wallabies hopping all over Connor's brother's garden than she was by Connor himself. Gorgeous muscular legs with a sprinkling of dark hairs; loose, lean body coiled watchfully in the armchair; tousled hair, unshaven face... It was as much as Zoe could do to keep breathing.

'You must be Zoe,' said a motherly woman on the screen. 'I hope Connor's made you comfortable in that house.'

'Of course I have,' said Connor, an edge to his voice. 'Zoe's my tenant and a midwife at the Medical Centre. I'd be daft not to.'

'Just checking, pet,' said his mother. 'We've been talking to young Jamie. He's a credit to you, love.'

'Thank you.' Zoe looked at the other people sitting in the garden with mugs or cans of drink. It looked as if it was well into the afternoon there. But there were so many of them! She identified Connor's brother easily, and his father was just an older version.

'You work with Connor?' said his father. 'How do you manage? I've always found him trouble.'

'Because you always think you know what's wrong with the NHS and you expect me to put it right.'

'See, Zoe? He's always arguing.'

She could feel the tension in Connor, but still Zoe would never have thought that a family could squabble so amiably when they were thousands of miles apart. 'It's nice to meet you,' she said to the screen, 'but I've got to give Jamie breakfast and get ready for work.'

'Thanks,' said Connor as he gave Jamie a piggyback to the coach house. 'You've stopped them nagging and provided them with something to talk about. I'm usually a disappointment because nothing happens to me.'

*Nothing apart from life-threatening diseases.* Aloud, she said, 'And whose fault is that? Jo's always saying you don't go to anything she arranges.'

He slanted her a sardonic look. 'She arranges things for *everyone*. I'm into solitary pursuits. Sorry if my family have made you late. They're a bit overwhelming en masse.'

'Connor, they were great! Do you know how lucky you are, how envious I am of you? I'd give anything for a family like that!'

He looked at her as if she needed her head examining. 'I remember you told me your mother lived in Jersey and you hardly saw her. Don't you ever go down for holidays?'

'No. Neil wasn't keen.' She paused, realising that her life had changed. She was the one in control now. She could afford to spend some of her pay on a trip to Jersey. She didn't have to do what Neil wanted all the time, clinging on to the illusion of family solidarity. 'We could go there now, couldn't we?' she said slowly. 'It would give Jamie a chance to get to know them. I'd like that.' She smiled at him. 'Thank you, Connor.'

He smiled back. And, just for a moment, there didn't seem to be anyone else in the world.

The vision of Zoe dressed only in a towel stayed with Connor well into morning surgery. He was beginning to think she was a lifesaver. He'd been so irritated when his mother and father had fetched the whole of the family outside to talk to 'Uncle Connor'. He *looked* as though he was over his illness, so why should he not be gathered back into the fold? They would never understand how unbearable it was for him to see his nephews and nieces and be so forcibly reminded of a way of life that he would never now have. So he'd been edgy and cross and his mother mentioning Zoe and Jamie and how she'd love to meet them had touched him on the raw.

But then he'd seen her leaning out of her window and had had a purely masculine reaction. He remembered what it was like when he was young, fancy free, and the summer turned hot and all the girls he knew started raising their hemlines. The rest of the video call wasn't nearly as aggravating.

He was a little taken aback at work, though, when a couple of people mentioned that he seemed to be in a good mood. Was he usually so unapproachable?

He buzzed for his next patient, reading the receptionist's brief notes. Alice Reynolds, forty-five years old, possibly suffering from gastric flu. She came into the room, pale and tired-looking, apologising for taking up his time.

He reassured her. 'Having our time taken up is what we're for.' He listened to her symptoms as he went though all the standard checks, noticing how she blanched when one of the receptionists went past his part-open door carrying a tray of fresh coffee. 'How is your health generally?' he asked, studying her medical history on his computer screen.

'It's normally fine. I thought maybe I'd eaten something dodgy—but food poisoning wouldn't go on this long, would it? That's why Tim told me to make the appointment. The poor man's had to cook his own breakfast for nearly a fortnight now. I just can't face anything fried.'

Connor's suspicions grew. 'I see you brought a sample with you. That was a good idea.'

'Do you know what it might be, then?'

'Maybe. Can you remember the date of your last period?'

'No, I've been really irregular the last few months. Slowing down, I thought, ready for The Change.' Then Alice's mouth dropped open as she realised what he was getting at. 'Oh, my goodness.'

'I take it pregnancy is a possibility, then. Are your breasts sore at all?'

'Um…yes, as a matter of fact, but… Golly, after all these years.'

Connor smiled. 'It happens surprisingly often. A whole bunch of your remaining eggs get released in one fell swoop. Nature's way of saying, *Get on with it*. We can test your urine here and have the result by this evening. Or, if you want to know faster, you can buy a kit from the chemist.'

'I want you to do it,' she said straight away. 'Superstition. I did so many of them when we were younger and they were all negative. I swore I'd never…' She gave a nervous laugh. 'Oh, dear, my legs have gone all shaky. I can't move. You'll know by this evening, you said?'

Connor made an instant decision. 'Normally, yes. But I do have some sample test kits here, so…'

He gave Alice a gentle examination while the indicator stick matured. 'It's positive,' he said, and watched the tremulous joy spread over her face.

'Oh, good heavens. Oh, good *heavens*! We never thought we would be. All these years… It's a gift. Tell me what to do. I won't remember anything, but tell me anyway.'

'I'll do better than that. I'll introduce you to Zoe Hilton, our practice midwife. She can give you the pregnancy handouts that we've put together. Did you drive here?'

'Yes, but I can't drive back. I'm all of a dither. A child. Oh, golly. I'll ring Tim to fetch me. He works just up the High Street—he's a solicitor. Oh, I can't wait to see his face.'

Connor pushed the phone across. 'Call him from here. I'll ask one of the receptionists to bring you a cup of tea while you wait. You can be in shock for nice reasons as well as nasty ones.'

Baby Clinic was finishing as he steered Alice back to the waiting room. He heard Zoe laughing with a couple of the mums and called her over. As she crossed the floor with an enquiring expression on her face, his heart skipped a beat. She might be in regulation uniform with a neatly pinned plait now, but she was just as gorgeous, just as full of life as when he'd seen her this morning with a towel wrapped around her and her hair twisted haphazardly up on her head.

Just as he'd explained about Alice being excited and a bit shocked at finding herself an elderly primigravida, the doors burst open and Tim Reynolds rushed in—closely followed by a broadly smiling Jo.

Tim raced across, having eyes for no one but his wife. 'Really, Alice? Are we really going to have a baby? After all this time?'

Alice nodded, her eyes bright with happy tears. 'We really are. Dr Maitland did the test himself. And this is Midwife Hilton, and she'll give us stuff to read and she's going to look after us every step of the way. Oh, Tim!'

'Oh, darling!'

They hugged each other, oblivious to the patients watching with fond smiles, oblivious to the receptionist trying to hand Alice a steaming mug. When they broke off, they were both crying.

'I'll be all right now,' said Alice. She flung her arms round Connor. 'Thank you so much.'

There was a general murmur of 'ahh' and a chorus of good wishes as they left hand in hand.

Jo came over, smiled at the two of them. 'Tim and Alice are old friends,' she said. 'This is the best news they've had in years. And I can't think of a better doctor and midwife to look after them than you two. I must go and tell Sam.'

Connor saw Zoe wipe her eyes. She fumbled for a tissue and looked up at him. 'Don't you *dare* ever tell me that being a GP isn't every bit as worthwhile as being a surgeon,' she said.

She moved across the room to chivvy the remaining Baby Clinic stragglers home. Connor remained where he was, feeling more than a bit emotional himself. Zoe was right—this was one of the reasons why he'd wanted to go into general practice all those years ago. And, just at this moment, there was nowhere else he wanted to be.

# CHAPTER SEVEN

JAMIE hopped up and down by the door, impatient to be off.

'Picnic, swimming things, change of clothes,' said Zoe, checking the bags. 'Come on, then.'

Jamie ran straight across Connor's lawn and in through the French windows, shouting, 'Uncle Connor! We're here!'

Zoe thought it might have been better to knock first but a voice called out, 'Come in. I'm almost ready.' And he appeared, looking truly wonderful in a pair of khaki shorts. 'Just one last email I need to send.'

While Connor's fingers danced across the keyboard, Zoe picked up a mangled magazine from the floor. A climbing magazine. 'Did this have an argument with the letter box?' she asked, smoothing it out. She just had time to read the words *Team secure funding for new route* underneath a photo of a jubilant group of climbers before Connor took it out of her hands and threw it into the waste paper basket.

'I've finished with it, anyway,' he said. 'Let's go.'

Zoe thought that his tone was unnecessarily short, but then he smiled and said, 'Looks like the weather man is being good to us,' and she felt happy again.

She followed him and Jamie out to the car. She was looking forward to the day as much as her son. So, she thought, was Connor. They had steered clear of personal conversations over the last two or three weeks, but she'd seen a definite change in him. He seemed more relaxed, still reserved but easier in his manner. He'd even started making jokes at work. Was it her influence? she wondered. She couldn't fail to notice his appreciative looks when—as now—she was wearing shorts and a fairly minimal T-shirt. She also couldn't disguise the fact that the little thrill every time she saw him never seemed to diminish, no matter how often they met.

Or maybe it was Jamie softening him. The boy adored him and had none of her reserve when asking for Connor's company. They were getting very close. Zoe didn't know how she felt about this. If Connor grew bored, didn't want to see so much of her son, then Jamie was going to be horribly hurt. She sighed, the butterflies in her stomach telling her that there might be a decision to be made some time in the near future. But what decision? And how to make it? For the moment she and Connor appeared to be in a semi-relationship partly based on her son. It was safe…but strangely unsatisfying.

For now, however, she was simply going to enjoy the day. Connor was going to teach her and Jamie how to canoe and neither of them was stupid enough to bring up emotional issues and spoil it.

Then her mobile rang.

Both Connor and Jamie stopped what they were doing and looked at her.

'It's all right,' she said, quite enjoying the twin expressions of wary alarm. 'It's my day off. Sheffield Maternity is just stuffed with midwives waiting for something to do.'

'Zoe? It's Paula Beskin. I think the baby is coming.'

Zoe blinked, thought back over her calendar. 'Paula? But you're not due for another three weeks. Are you sure? How often are the contractions?'

'Every ten minutes now; I've timed them. They've suddenly sped up. And the pain is getting worse, though it's not too bad yet. I'm doing the relaxation exercises.' There was a moment's silence and then Paula said in a small voice, 'I'm sorry, but can I still have the baby at home?'

Zoe thought rapidly. Sheffield Maternity was *not* stuffed with midwives ready to come out to a home delivery. But Paula was a sensible girl, there hadn't been any contra-indications at any of her appointments and a thirty-seven week baby was certainly viable. 'I'll be there as soon as I can,' she said, bidding a silent farewell to her lovely day. 'If there's an emergency before I arrive, head straight for the hospital and ring me on the way.' She shut off her phone with a sigh.

'Oh, *Mummy*.' Jamie's eyes had filled with tears.

Zoe crouched down. 'I'm sorry,' she said. 'That's the trouble with babies. They come when they feel like it. And I promised Paula a home delivery. It's at that farm where you saw the pigs and the hens, remember?' She kissed his forehead. 'I'll take you to play with Auntie Jo for the day. We'll go canoeing another time.'

Connor cleared his throat. 'Or Jamie and I can go on our own,' he said quietly. 'If you trust me with him. But I'll miss you.'

He'd miss her? She had a quiet shiver of pleasure at that. It meant he hadn't just been thinking of giving Jamie a nice day out today. But what he was suggesting was really big. Jamie playing football on the lawn or in the play dell with Connor was one thing; the pair of them going off alone to a large body of water was something else entirely.

Connor was regarding her steadily, not hassling, not pushing. 'I promise I'll take as much care of him as if he was my own s—that is, as if he was one of my nephews and nieces.'

'Please, Mummy? I'll be really good,' said a breathless voice.

Thoughts chased each other through Zoe's head. Connor had told her he'd taken his sisters' children canoeing several times. Jamie could swim like a fish. But…but… She took a deep breath. 'That would be wonderful,' she said, struggling not to sound completely paranoid.

She was a little peeved at the glee Jamie showed as he scrambled into the car without her, but then thought of the contrast between this excited little lad and the withdrawn child he had been in London. And, of course, she and Connor both had mobile phones and could keep in touch.

Connor squeezed her hand. 'Join us if you've got time,' he said.

She phoned Jo as she hurried back to the house to change.

'It's your call,' Jo said. 'Any problem, phone an ambulance and let me know. Or I'll get a doctor out there if need be. Not that I know one as competent as you.'

Within a very few minutes Zoe was getting her midwife bag out of the locked cupboard under the stairs. And, just in case, she put her shorts and T-shirt in the car too.

All the way to High Peak Farm, one question ran through Zoe's head. They could easily go to the reservoir another day. It wasn't going to dry up; the club wasn't going to scuttle all its canoes overnight. So why was she so disappointed? And the answer was there, just waiting for her to acknowledge it. It scared her rigid.

Because she would have been spending the whole day with Connor. And now she wasn't.

If all births were like this one, then Zoe would have wanted them all to take place at home. Paula's bedroom was on the ground floor, all the unnecessary clutter removed, next door to a bathroom. There should be no trouble, although she reminded herself that whenever she'd relied on there being no trouble there usually was. She remembered the old nursing mantra: Hope for the best and expect the worst.

Paula's mother greeted her. Zoe liked her at once, a very sensible lady. 'I'm going to stay here for the next few nights,' she said. 'Ask if you need anything, but I won't interfere. Luke's in with Paula; I've just been cleaning up a bit.'

Zoe looked round the living room. Cleaning up a bit? She wished most hospital wards were as clean as this. She decided that this was going to be a good birth.

And it was—a textbook birth, one that went right all the way through. There was a supportive, loving father-to-be; a mum-to-be who had been to all the classes, had done everything asked of her; Paula's mother as the perfect backup, tea and sandwiches or soup on demand. The soap, towels, extra bedding, all carefully ready. When Zoe walked into the bathroom she felt she needed dark glasses, the place sparkled so much.

A lot of the time in a birth was spent waiting. Zoe had time to read two texts from Connor. One said they'd arrived and the water was warm. The next said Jamie had paddled all by himself in a straightish line without a disaster.

Then there was the birth, and Paula had her little girl. It was an easy delivery—the father looked much more wrung-out than the mother—and, after the usual checks, Zoe felt quite happy to leave them. 'She's a lovely little girl and you're very lucky. You've got my mobile number. Any problems, any time, night or day, phone me. I'll be back tomorrow to have a look at you. I imagine you'll all spend most of the time before then asleep!'

'Everything will be okay,' said Paula's mother. Zoe had learned earlier that she had five children—all born at home.

Connor had told her where they would be canoeing. Near the car park and boat centre there was a beach across which a stream ran into the reservoir. The perfect place for a beginner. She drove to the car park, changed out of her uniform and walked to where she knew they would be.

She'd had a good day so far—not the day she had anticipated but still pretty good. Every time she delivered a baby, she felt emotional and happy. She'd enjoyed it even before she'd been a mother herself but, since having Jamie, births had been extra special. Now she just wanted to be with her son. And perhaps with Connor. She didn't really mind if there wasn't time for her to try canoeing herself.

She walked down the steep path towards the beach, smiling as she saw Connor and Jamie below her. They were both in hired canoes. Jamie in a tiny red plastic canoe, a red life jacket strapped round him, paddling furiously. And Connor behind him in a larger blue canoe. They were shouting at each other, obviously having a great time. Zoe felt a great welling up of happiness.

She couldn't believe what she saw next. Connor dug his paddle deep into the water, surged forward and drove the bows of his canoe into the side of Jamie's. There was a squeal from Jamie, his canoe capsized and suddenly he was under water.

All the air rushed out of Zoe's lungs in terror. She hadn't even realised she was running until she dodged to avoid someone coming towards the car park. How long had it been? What if he…? He might… But then his little head surfaced; he was all right! He splashed his way to the beach and crawled out of the water.

Zoe dashed down the last few feet of the path and ran across the beach. She grabbed the wet little figure, hugged him to her. He was never going in the water again. Never, never, never. 'Jamie, are you all right? I saw what happened and I just couldn't…'

'Did you see, Mummy? Did you see?' He pushed her away, looked past her and shouted, 'Uncle Connor, I did it! Did I do it right?'

She turned to see Connor behind her. Panic turned uncontrollably to anger. 'Are you mad? What were you thinking of? He could have drowned. Is this the way you behave with him when I'm not here? This is the last time I leave him alone with you.'

She knew her voice was shrill, her body trembling, but there was nothing she could do about it. The moment her son had disappeared under the water, it felt as if her heart had stopped.

Connor had been smiling to see her, but her words acted like a slap in the face. The light died out of his eyes. His voice was cold as he said, 'For goodness' sake, calm down, Zoe. You're upsetting him. Stop having hysterics and try thinking before you shout any more. Jamie was perfectly safe. One of the first things you have to learn when you start canoeing is how to free yourself if you capsize. We've been practising for the past hour. This was just a test and Jamie passed it perfectly—as I knew he would.'

'He didn't know he was going to capsize! You came up behind him.'

'You don't usually get a warning if you capsize by accident.'

'Didn't I do it right, Mummy?' Jamie's voice was tearful.

He was upset! For a moment, Zoe hated Connor fiercely for being right, but she hated herself more for overreacting so monumentally. She pulled her ragged emotions together before answering more calmly. 'You did it perfectly, darling. You did very well indeed. I'm so proud of you.' It took a tremendous effort, but she went on. 'You'll…you'll have to show me how to do that when I learn.'

'Show you now.'

'No!' She took a deep breath. 'Just show me how you paddle.'

She saw Connor looking at her; he nodded and held his hand out to Jamie. The two of them pulled the little canoe ashore, turned it over to drain the water from it. She heard Jamie say, 'That was good, wasn't it, Uncle Connor?'

She watched as Connor held the canoe steady for Jamie, watched as they paddled together a little way out and then back again. She kept an encouraging smile on her face, but she just couldn't reconcile the two emotions warring inside her. First, her heart was still pounding at the thought that

Jamie had been in danger. But, second, she was pleased to see how happy he was to be with Connor. What was she to feel?

Connor brought Jamie back and said neutrally, 'I think that's probably enough for today. Why don't you dry Jamie and get him dressed—our stuff is over there on the table. And I'll take the canoes back to the boat centre.'

Hardly able to speak, overcome by emotion, she nodded. Connor slipped into his own canoe, tied Jamie's canoe to it and paddled off. He was a physical man, she thought. His every action was graceful, economical. It was difficult not to admire the way his canoe forged through the water, overtaking a couple of shrieking, splashing teenagers, who tried to race him—and didn't succeed.

She dried Jamie, dressed him, held him in her arms. And, not surprisingly, he fell asleep. There was comfort in holding the little body. But she had to think what to say when Connor returned.

Twenty minutes later he was back, his face the careful mask it had been when she'd first met him. In a low voice she said, 'Connor, I owe you an apology. I was wrong and I'm sorry. I should have known you better. But when I think Jamie might be in danger, reason just goes out the window. I remember…and…' She didn't want to say any more; she was afraid that the tears might flow.

He sat by her side, briefly stroked Jamie's hair. 'Shh. I was wrong to jump down your throat. I was hurt that you'd misjudged me. You love him; you were being a mother, that was all.' Then he smiled, and she smiled tremulously back, and suddenly things were several degrees better. He went on, 'It excuses most things.'

'It doesn't excuse me hurting you when you've curtailed half the things you would normally have done today just to keep him safe. Sometimes I say things before I consider whether it's a good idea or not.'

'Perhaps that makes you a more honest person.' He reached for the picnic bag, peered inside and said, 'Coffee and sandwiches left. Are you hungry?'

Yes, she was. She hadn't realised. She shifted Jamie against her shoulder and took the cheese roll he handed her.

'Zoe, I do understand your reaction whenever you think Jamie is in danger. Even though you're a sensible, unflappable midwife, able to assess situations calmly—as soon as Jamie is at the slightest risk, you immediately remember the car crash and him only escaping by a miracle. That's it, isn't it?'

She nodded, feeling miserable.

He gave her arm a brief squeeze. 'It's natural,' he said. 'The more you let him do—the more you trust him to do safely—the easier it will get.'

'You mean I've got *years* of scary pastimes ahead of me? Oh, goody.'

Connor laughed. 'I'm afraid he does seem to be an active sort of child. But surely that's better than keeping him in cotton wool at home all the time?'

'True. I saw plenty of older brothers and sisters in London who only ever went out of doors to go shopping or to school. The parents didn't see anything wrong with keeping them occupied with the telly or the computer. Jamie and I used to go to the park or the swimming pool or the soft-play gym as often as we could.'

'It's a pity more people don't do that. I promise that he'll be as safe as it's possible to be within reasonable limits when he's with me. I'm the last person in the world to endanger a child.'

Zoe looked up, alerted by the note of deep feeling in his voice.

'Why?' she asked.

'Because children are a gift. And so many people don't appreciate them.' His voice had gone remote. He nodded across to the small beach where families were dotted about, dogs and children scampering in and out of the water. 'A lot of people get a pet dog from Animal Rescue. People abandon dogs; Animal Rescue tries to find them a good home. But you don't just go and get a dog by asking. They send an inspector round; he checks your home, your background, your suitability. He does his job conscientiously and quite a few people are turned down.'

'What are you saying, Connor?'

'That people can have babies without ever having the checks that a stray dog gets. It doesn't seem fair, does it? That couple the other week—Alice and Tim Reynolds. They would have passed the children checklist with ease—yet it took until it was nearly too late for Alice to become pregnant. Barbara and Roy Reagan, on the other hand, have had two kids in quick succession and are finding it difficult to cope.'

'Life isn't fair, Connor. Would you really want to live in the sort of state-controlled environment where you had to pass an exam before you were allowed to have babies? No, of course you wouldn't. That's why people like us exist—to give help and advice along the way.'

He smiled at her and she felt she could forgive him anything. 'You're right. Sorry for sounding off. Sometimes I get frustrated about situations that I can do nothing about.'

'I'm flattered that with me you can say what you feel.'

'You know,' he said thoughtfully, 'thinking of work again, ideally I'd like to have Barbara's husband as a patient too.'

Zoe was startled. 'But he's an awkward, argumentative so-and-so. No doctor wants a patient like that.'

'It's easier to treat the whole family rather than just one person in it. And I think I understand Roy a bit. Basically, he's just an immature lad who needs help to grow up.'

'You are a good doctor, Connor. I'll try and get Barbara to persuade her husband to come back to us next time I see her. And we'll add a list of local birth-through-teen activities to the pregnancy pack with an advisory note for people to use them. Anything else on your wish list?'

He gave a short laugh. 'Oh, just put a notice up on the surgery wall telling people to take a little extra care in knowing more about who they are going to marry. That should help too.'

Zoe suddenly felt cold. And hurt. 'Was that a dig at me?' she demanded. 'We all make mistakes, Connor.'

He looked at her in consternation. 'What? No! Oh, hell, Zoe—I would never dream of… I was talking about me.'

At last. He'd been jolted into revealing something of himself. Zoe knew if she didn't press him now, he'd slide away again. 'You? What do you mean?'

'Is Jamie heavy? You can't manage to hold him and drink coffee at the same time. Would you like me to take him?'

'No, I want you to stop hiding, Connor. I've told you my tragedy. I want you to tell me yours.'

There was a long silence. 'That magazine this morning,' he began.

This morning seemed like a hundred years ago to Zoe, but she nodded. 'The mangled one?'

'Quick, aren't you? There was a photograph of a climbing team who are going to attempt a prestigious new route. It will be exciting, dangerous, challenging—all the things I used to revel in.'

'I'm sorry you can't climb that well any more,' said Zoe.

He looked at her in slight surprise. 'I'm misleading you. That's not why I threw it away. One of the team was my ex-girlfriend. She's a very bright doctor, fearless on a rock face…' His voice tailed off.

Zoe sipped her coffee and waited.

'We seemed very suited. I assumed we'd eventually get married, bring up a little pack of rock climbers of our own, and live happily ever after. It turned out I was missing a couple of facts. One was that, for a doctor, she had a surprising amount of trouble coping with seriously ill people in her own life. And two…'

He swallowed, his eyes stony and lost as he stared out over the reservoir. Zoe put down the Thermos cup and folded her hand over his clenched fist.

'She left me when I was ill. She'd had the offer of a US-based job, but I think with hindsight she'd have left me anyway. A while later I got a letter from her. I guess she knew I wasn't up to emails at the time. It said she hoped I was getting better, she was really enjoying her new post, and that the climbing in Yosemite was fabulous.'

Zoe winced when she saw the expression on his face. She knew Connor was a self-controlled man; he didn't like to let his emotions show. But they showed now. He was angry—but most of all he was hurting. She took his hand in both hers, but said nothing.

It was a while before he spoke, and when he did his voice was clipped, monotonous. Though he was looking at her, she knew his eyes were unseeing.

'She also said that perhaps I should know now that a few days after she had arrived in San Francisco she'd discovered that she was pregnant. But I didn't need to worry. She'd organised things; the foetus was gone. She'd been pregnant with our child—my child! But, Zoe, she'd aborted it! How could she?'

Zoe's eyes filled with tears. 'Oh, Connor,' she whispered. She'd heard him talk of his nephews and nieces. She knew how he was with Jamie. The news that a child of his own had been disposed of so casually must have nearly killed him. 'Oh, Connor, I'm so sorry.'

'It…it didn't help with my recovery.'

'I should imagine not.'

'I'd accepted that because I was…damaged…Francine no longer loved me enough to stick around. I could cope with that—just—by blocking all thoughts of her. But that she should care so little for our unborn child that she would… Well, that just about finished me off.'

'Oh, Connor,' said Zoe again. She lifted his hand to her mouth and kissed it without thinking.

'So can you understand now why I tend not to trust people? Even worse, not to trust my own judgement?'

Zoe stared at him. There was so much that she wanted to say, so much that she wanted to tell him about trust…but was she the right person to do so? His case was so similar to her own. She had to say something. 'Connor, I know that…'

But he'd had enough talking for a while. He turned away, started to pack up their bags. In a totally different voice, he said, 'I'll take these up to the car and then come back to give you a hand with Jamie.'

He was away longer than the task would normally take and she thought she knew why. Connor didn't like revealing himself. And for a while his feelings would be too strong to suppress.

When he returned, Jamie was stirring. Connor lifted him into his arms. 'Time to go home, young man. We'll do it all another day.'

Zoe stood up, looking at her son cradled against Connor's chest and seeing the bleak pain hidden behind Connor's now deliberately casual manner. She put her hand on his arm, feeling the warmth and the strength of the man. 'She wasn't right for you, Connor. I know what she did must have hurt un-bearably, but…'

*But it was my child.* Zoe heard it as clearly as if he'd said it aloud.

She tried again. 'You mustn't think all people are the same. Life can be different; there are happy couples. Look at Jo and Sam.'

His dark blue eyes rested on her for a moment. 'I told you before about having had Lyme disease, didn't I?'

She nodded.

'And you being you, knowing nothing about the disease, you looked it up?'

Time for honesty. 'Yes,' she confessed. 'I wanted to…know about you.'

'Did you read all about the possible side effects, the possible consequences?' His voice was harsh again.

'Yes.' Suddenly, Zoe had a terrible suspicion about what he was about to say next. 'Connor, you're not…?'

'I am. I'm infertile. I've always loved children. And I've lost the only chance I ever had of having a child of my own. Maybe life can be different for some people, Zoe. But not for me.'

# CHAPTER EIGHT

THE invitation arrived at the surgery the next morning. A stiff cream card, the wording in embossed silver.

> *Mr and Mrs T Reynolds would like to invite Ms Z Hilton and partner to the Summer Ball at Cantwell House.*

In a fortnight's time. A ball? She blinked, and went to see Jo.

Jo grinned and waved a similar card at her. 'Sam and I are invited too; we go every year. It's a charity ball organised by the local solicitors' association. It's Buckley's most prestigious social event. Pictures in the paper and everything. You'll have a great time; we can share a table.'

'But I haven't been to a ball in years. My ball-going days are long over. And why would they invite me?'

'You're invited because Alice and Tim think you've been so helpful with the pregnancy. It's never too late to restart. You used to love dancing.'

Zoe felt a momentary touch of sadness. Yes, she used to love to dance. Before Neil started to…

'There's another thing,' Jo went on. 'There were three invitations. Connor got one too.'

'Connor!'

'Why not? Alice thinks he's a wonderful doctor. She also thinks he's kind and thoughtful—which he is. And his invitation will say *Dr C Maitland and partner*.' Jo looked expectantly at her friend. 'Why not go as a couple? Just for the ball, of course.'

'No! I just don't do dancing any more, and I suspect neither does Connor. We get on all right at the moment; he's very fond of Jamie and Jamie thinks he's marvellous.'

'I know; I've seen them together. Every child needs a father figure.'

'Jo, don't go there!'

'I'm not going anywhere. Just re-telling a well known fact. Now, just supposing, just perhaps, Connor asks you to go to the ball as his partner. Would you go?'

'He won't ask!'

'All I'm doing is asking you to suppose!'

'Well, I'd think about it. Now I've got work to do.' And Zoe fled from Jo's office, her thoughts in turmoil.

She had been climbing with Connor, canoeing with him, saw him with Jamie in his garden most evenings. They got on well and they were easier round each other since that day at the reservoir. But, despite the undoubted attraction between them, they both recognised that there was little they could do about it. Both had their demons still to fight.

But she used to love dancing. And something, perhaps the way he was so light on his feet, told her that Connor would be a great dancer. It might be nice if, just for one night, they could forget the reasons keeping them apart and just enjoy being together.

That evening Connor sat in his study, for the fifth time took the invitation from his pocket and read it. The message hadn't changed. *Dr C Maitland and partner*... And partner?

His first reaction had been to write a courteous note of

regret. Since he'd been in Buckley he had received more than a few invitations to social gatherings and had refused them all. He was a doctor and was happy to meet and help people—professionally. In his own time he liked his own company. He didn't have a partner, didn't want one, didn't intend to go to any function where he'd have to dance, chat or otherwise act like a social animal. He was happy the way he was.

And yet…

That morning he had been standing next to Jo when they picked up their mail. He'd seen that she had received the same invitation as he had; they'd opened them at the same time. 'Party invitation,' she'd said. 'As usual, I guess you won't be going, Connor?'

'I doubt it. Not my style.'

'Pity; it's usually a good do. It looks as if there's an invitation for Zoe too. I doubt she'll go either. She used to love dancing, though she hasn't done any for ages. Well, to work.' And she had walked away.

He had felt slightly aggrieved that she'd been so certain he'd refuse the invitation. Was he so predictable? So set in his ways? If he wanted to go to the ball, then he would. Wouldn't he? And it would make sense if…

'Uncle Connor?' a small voice shouted from outside. He had left the French windows of his living room open, left his study door open—he realised he had done so in order to hear when Jamie came into his garden.

'Coming,' he shouted, stuffing the invitation into his pocket. There was Jamie, smiling proudly, a sheet of paper in his hand. Behind him was Zoe, a more hesitant smile on her face. It was a warm evening; she was dressed as so often in T-shirt and shorts. And she looked well.

There was the flash of pleasure he always felt when he saw her. And another, almost foreign feeling. A memory, even. He wondered what it would be like to dance with her. To hold her in his arms, to feel her body touching, moving against his. To smell her perfume, perhaps to rest his cheek against hers. Jo had said that Zoe used to like dancing. So had he. But dancing with Francine, he reminded himself. And, to his surprise, for the first time in years he was able to think of what she'd done without a burst of bitterness.

Francine was out of his life now. But, despite his words the other day, he was learning that he still had a life to lead. One that maybe included Zoe? He didn't know.

'Uncle Connor, I've drawed a picture of me and you and Miss Jones said it was very good and be sure to show you. It was when we were canoeing.'

Connor knelt on the grass to study the drawing.

'That's you in the blue canoe and me in the red one. And I'm falling out because it's an accident.'

Zoe had been so furious with him. And he'd been furious with her for not seeing that he had Jamie's best interests at heart. He looked up into the child's expectant face. 'That's very good, Jamie. Know what I'm going to do? I'm going to take this to my computer and copy it. Then you'll have this on your fridge and I'll have a copy on mine.'

'Fantastic! I'm going on the swings now.' And Jamie rushed off, leaving him to face Zoe.

'Come in while I copy this,' he said. 'Jamie will be fine for a moment on his own.'

'All right. But not for long.' She made a face at her own reluctance. 'I'm getting used to leaving him—but it's still hard.'

'You're a good mother.'

She followed him into the study, was silent as he turned on the scanner and placed Jamie's picture against the glass plate. Then, when it started humming, he took the invitation out of his pocket and showed it to her. 'I gather you have one of these?'

She hesitated, looked at him warily. 'Yes, I have. Why?'

'Are you thinking of going? Jo said you used to love dancing.'

'I did. But that was then and this is now. I haven't danced for years. I don't like to upset Alice and Tim, but I think I'll have to refuse.'

'I quite liked dancing too. And for me it feels like a lifetime. I was going to refuse, but then I wondered…' His voice trailed away.

She bowed her head slightly; he could see a slight blush on her cheeks. Then she lifted her head, looked at him steadily, the pinkness in her cheeks still showing. 'Connor, if you're going to ask me to go to the ball as your partner, then do it. And, before you do, just to stop any potential embarrassment, let me tell you that, if you do, I'll say yes.'

'Really?'

'Yes. I'd like to go to the ball with you. It'll be one demon less for me, but only if I go with someone I trust.' She gave a small smile. 'I think it would be good for both of us, come to that. This can be one night apart. For a night I'll be Cinderella.'

'Will a taxi do instead of a golden coach?'

'Well, only just.'

'Then, Cinders, will you accompany a shop-worn prince to the ball?'

'There's nothing shop-worn about you, Connor. Did you know you should smile more often? When you do, the whole world seems to sparkle.'

He took a step towards her, took her hands in his. They were friends now—and very nearly something more. He knew she wouldn't move if he kissed her. In fact, he thought she might like it. So…

From outside a voice called, 'Uncle Connor, can we play football now?'

And it was she who reached up to kiss him on his cheek. 'We're making progress,' she said. 'But I still don't know where we're going.'

* * *

Zoe shooed her butterflies away and decided that she was really looking forward to the occasion. For the moment, worries about her relationship with Connor were shelved. What she was interested in was an evening of dressing up, dancing and having a good time. Just one evening. It was something she hadn't done for quite a while. Towards the end of her marriage to Neil they had been to fewer and fewer events together. He always got drunk, wouldn't listen to reason... She preferred to stay at home with Jamie.

So what would she wear? She'd been living in either casual clothes or her uniform ever since she'd moved up here. She went through her wardrobe, thinking that the smart clothes she possessed seemed to belong in a different life. She was shocked when she came to the black dress she'd bought for Neil's funeral. It was a good one, quite expensive. She'd felt she'd owed it to the memory of those early years when he'd swept her off her feet and made her feel as if she was the most exciting woman in the universe. How things had changed. She sat on her bed with the dress in her lap and remembered her feelings when she had worn it at the funeral. There had been a mixture of anger and sadness and guilt. Anger still at his immense irresponsibility, anger at his endangering their child. Sadness for the man he had been; the man who wouldn't change. Guilt because of the shameful relief that one part of her life was over.

She blotted her eyes, knowing she could never wear the dress again—the same feelings would rise up in her. She wasn't even sure why she'd kept it. She reached for a large pair of scissors. Then she held back. It would be a pointless gesture to cut it up. Neil and life with him were now behind her. She had a new life, a different future. Somebody else would value this dress. She would ask Jo, who knew everybody, if she could find a discreet home for it.

But what was she to wear?

She gave the dress to Jo the next day, telling her briskly that she and Connor had discussed the ball and would go together.

'Good heavens! I mean, how lovely.'

'Just as friends, Jo.'

'Absolutely. Just friends.'

But there was a look in Jo's eyes that told Zoe it was time to distract her. 'I've not been to a posh do for ages and I'm at a bit of a loss. I don't know the local shops very well and I…'

'Oh, gosh, of course you don't. First, book a hair appointment. You want either Mary or Jane at MaryJane's in that little street behind the church. They're the best in Buckley. Be sure to tell them that you work here. Sam helped Mary over a bad spell a couple of years ago and they've both been grateful ever since.' She thought a minute. 'Dress…Go to Top Two Toe at the bottom of the High Street. A bit expensive but well worth it. This might be a small town but people here appreciate good stuff. And tell them that…'

'Tell them that I'm from Buckley Medical Centre,' Zoe finished for her. 'I will.'

As the date came closer she found that she was really looking forward to it. She was looking forward to dressing up, to having a glass or two of champagne, to dancing again. She was glad Connor wasn't one of those men who resolutely refused to dance. She would, of course, take the floor with whoever asked her, but dancing with Connor would be lovely. When the day of the ball came she realised she had been waiting for it like a child waited for Christmas. They were in luck; it was sunny all day and the night promised to be warm but not too hot. Connor had arranged a taxi. Jamie, his best teddy and his *Big Red Tractor* book had been installed in a corner of Jo's daughters' bedroom, with their favourite baby-sitter to look after them all. All was well.

Zoe had come back home to get ready. The taxi would pick her and Connor up from her house. Now she was sitting on her patio waiting for Connor to walk across the garden. She had asked him to come over a little early. On the patio table were two glasses and a chilled bottle of Prosecco. They were both going to find it awkward to enter the ballroom this evening. She thought they might have a glass of wine before they set off. She laced her fingers together, then unlaced them. Why was she nervous?

'Stop that,' she told herself. 'You know perfectly well why.'

Connor. Pure and simple. It was all very well to say to Jo that they were just friends. The truth was that she was comfortable in his company, she trusted him with Jamie; she was starting to trust him with herself. That thought alone was enough to make her wonder where their friendship might be heading. The longer their acquaintance went on, the easier it became to think that maybe it was possible to have a relationship without getting hurt. She stared down at her hands. Very deliberately, she took the wedding ring off the third finger of her left hand—and placed it on her right hand. Perhaps, in time, she would stop wearing it completely. But it was a big step.

Then she saw him walking along his path and opening the gate. It took her a moment to register that in his formal dinner jacket Connor looked more gorgeous than she had ever seen him. As happened so often, her heart started beating faster.

Connor fumbled with the catch on the gate between his garden and Zoe's. He could feel his heart speed up and wished it wouldn't. He wanted to remain calm, didn't want any kind of excess emotion.

This was exactly the kind of event he had been avoiding. He'd been to too many charity balls with Francine when they had been a golden couple—dining, dancing, partying, surrounded by friends who lived the same way. Working hard, playing harder. When he'd taken his dinner jacket to be drycleaned he had found in the inside pocket an invitation to *Dr*

*C Maitland and Guest* to a reception at the Savoy. He had torn the card in half, wishing he could get rid of the memories as easily.

But what he was feeling now had nothing to do with the past. Anticipation had crept up on him without warning and he was actively looking forward to this ball. He was honest enough to acknowledge that the reason was Zoe.

What was he to do about her? Just how far could he let her into his life? For that matter, just how far would she allow *him* into *her* life? Over the past few weeks they had become closer, but did he want to take it to the next stage?

He had loved Francine, trusted her, and she had let him down in such a way that he had doubted he would ever love or trust again. But Zoe was different. He already knew she was loyal, but there was more to it than that, much more. She stirred his senses. Her smile lifted him with its warmth and all-encompassing humanity. He found himself trying to make her smile on purpose.

He latched the gate behind him, turned and saw her sitting on the patio. His breath caught in his throat. She was wonderful! She had let her hair down; it trailed over bare shoulders. Her dress was apparently simple, fashioned in peach silk. The bodice clung, enhancing the brownness of her bare arms. The skirt was what he would describe as swirly, fuller than the bodice; he guessed it was bought specifically with dancing in mind. Strappy sandals peeped out below the skirt.

As he drew nearer he noticed she was wearing jewellery. A necklace of amber hung low on her neck, dangling gold earrings replaced the neat studs that she normally wore.

'You look absolutely marvellous,' he said, and heard the shake in his voice. He couldn't help himself; he bent over and kissed her lightly on the cheek. He felt her shock, but when she raised her eyes to his they were pleased.

'You look pretty good yourself,' she said. 'I bought a bottle of Prosecco. I thought we had time for just one drink before the taxi arrives. Will you open it?'

He sat opposite, puzzling over the slight anxiety he could hear in her voice. 'Are you nervous?' he asked in disbelief, easing off the cork and filling the two glasses.

'A bit. I used to go to grand parties with Neil before he…' She broke off. 'The thing is—these past few weeks I've been building a new life, a more stable one. Oh, I love being Cinderella and dressing up, but I suppose I'm a little worried that memories from the past might spoil tonight. Silly, really.'

'Not silly at all. I had a few similar thoughts myself. Let's make a pact—tonight, neither of us is to think of anything except the present. Time out, as it were. After all, Cinderella wasn't worried that at midnight the coach and horses would turn back into a pumpkin and rats. She went ahead and enjoyed herself anyway.' Connor leaned forward and clinked his glass against hers. 'To a wonderful evening to come.'

'One night of magic?' She laughed uncertainly, then bit her lip and studied his face. 'All right; you've convinced me. To a wonderful evening to come.'

They both sipped; Connor felt the bubbles tickle his throat. Tonight, he decided extravagantly, whatever he could give Zoe, she would have.

If a magic night needed a magic setting, then Zoe thought Cantwell House was it. She, Connor, Jo and Sam were taken to the ballroom and shown to a table. A bottle of champagne in a silver bucket stood on it. Behind them was a wall of French windows, opening out to the terrace and a view of the gardens beyond.

Zoe looked around the beautiful sparkling room and smiled. She was going to enjoy herself. She was with friends, all of whom were out to have a good time. And she was with a man who… No, she wouldn't think about the future. They had agreed. Today was for today.

'You look like you used to,' Sam said to her. 'Radiant. Buckley must be good for you.'

'Something is certainly good for me,' Zoe said. 'I feel especially happy tonight.' She hoped that Jo and Sam hadn't noticed the look that Connor gave her.

And then a band started to play.

'Sam,' said Jo, 'we're dancing. If only to prove to you that those ballroom dancing lessons were worth it.'

'Too right. They won't play the old stuff for long.' He cleared his throat. 'My dear, may I have the pleasure of this dance?'

'But certainly; I'd be delighted.' Jo winked at Zoe and Connor. 'He can still impress when he wants.' They glided across the floor.

'Would you like to dance, Zoe?' asked Connor.

'I'd love to dance.' As she stood, suddenly Zoe felt shy.

This was the first time Connor had had his arm round her in a not-just-for-comfort way. It was unsettling and exciting both at the same time. They were close together; she could smell the faint fragrance of his cologne, feel the warmth of his body. She rested her hand on the silk of his dinner jacket. Her eyes were drawn to his. Had Cinderella felt this way?

They danced. There was that initial hesitation while they learned just how their bodies would move together, worked out how to lead, how to follow. But they seemed to fall into a rhythm almost at once. They danced as if they had been made for each other. Zoe gave herself to the music and the consciousness that she was in Connor's arms.

'You're a very good dancer,' she told him.

'I used to do a lot of it. But I never enjoyed it as much as I am doing now.'

'That's a lovely thing to say. Can we stay on the floor for the next dance?'

He smiled down at her, directly into her eyes. 'Tonight, your wish is my command.'

Of course they couldn't come to the ball and simply dance all evening. Apart from the fact that this was meant to be a social occasion, it would cause far too much speculation. So they sat at their table for a while, drank champagne and chatted to friends who came by. She was asked to dance by other people she'd met since she'd moved up. She remembered that thrill of knowing she was in demand. There was also a distinctly guilty pleasure in seeing the envious glances of the other girls when they recognised her partner.

'All the women's eyes are on you,' she said to Connor. 'People are jealous of me, and I feel sneakily pleased.'

'I think it's more likely that all eyes are on you. I'm just another man in a penguin suit. Come on, let's dance again. There's a registrar from the hospital moving towards us and I know he wants to ask you to dance—but I want it more.'

Zoe laughed and let herself be pulled into the throng. The music was more modern now, so the dance floor was crowded. The temperature rose along with the noise level. Connor asked if she'd like to walk in the gardens to cool down. Others were doing the same. It was dusk, but there were discreet lights scattered around, illuminating the paths.

She thought that a walk in the gardens would be lovely. As they walked to the far end of the terrace she took his arm, and became aware that he was guiding her away from most of the others. Was this the old Connor wanting solitude? Her senses told her probably not. And, as she thought it, a frisson of expectation ran through her.

They walked along a dimly lit path, the warm air heavy with the mingled scents of Cantwell House's famous old-fashioned roses and the drifts of white and pink nicotiana along the borders.

They came to a bench, dark and secluded, and they sat,

hands just touching. Zoe looked up and found that he was looking down at her. In the moonlight he seemed even more magnificent than by day.

'Is this still our evening out of time, Cinderella?' he asked in a low voice.

She smiled, felt herself shiver. 'Oh, yes,' she whispered.

Being kissed by Connor was magical. At first the touch of his lips was delicate, tentative even, but as her body pressed closer to his, he became more assertive. She felt his finger-tips trail across her naked shoulders and when they moved gently over the swell of her breasts she could detect that they were trembling. She wanted to stay here for ever being kissed by him; she was being transported into a realm where she didn't know what might…

In the distance there was a fanfare of trumpets. Shaken back to the present, she could hear the sound of feet on gravel. People were chattering loudly, coming towards them up the path. Zoe felt cheated when Connor took his arms from round her and leant back against the stone of the bench. He kept hold of one of her hands, though.

'Perhaps we ought to get back,' he said, his voice husky with disappointment. 'This place is getting too popular.'

She felt better, knowing that he wanted to stay as much as she did. 'I suppose so,' she said. She found a grin. 'But I'm still Cinderella and it's not midnight yet.'

He smiled back at her. 'Now that is good news.' They walked back hand in hand. Whether it was the champagne or the moonlight or the fairy lights, Zoe no longer cared.

Back in the ballroom, they discovered that the fanfare was because the buffet was being served. Much to her amaze-ment, Zoe found she was hungry. But then she'd packed quite a lot into the past three or four hours.

The buffet, like everything else organised so far, was superb. She picked smoked salmon on rye biscuits with cream cheese, ham vol-au-vents, chicken in a rich cream sauce. To the side, a tossed rocket salad.

'I'm eating the salad because it's slimming,' she told Connor. 'I'm eating the rest because tonight I'm just not bothered.'

He chuckled. 'Leave some space for the pudding.'

She looked at the exotic fruit salads, the cream cakes, the ice creams. 'I will,' she said.

They returned to their table to eat and chat some more. Jo phoned the babysitter to check that all was well. Empty plates were cleared away by efficient waiters. Coffee was served. Then, from the stage at the end of the ballroom, there was a welcome and a couple of short speeches. And all the time Zoe was aware of Connor next to her, the scent of him, the brush of his arm against hers, the warm pressure of his thigh. She'd been glad to sit down and eat, but now she felt energised and impatient. She wanted to dance with Connor again. Or go for another stroll in that magical garden. Most of all, she wanted to kiss him and dissolve in his arms again.

The band struck up again. 'I think you need some quiet, floating around time,' said Connor, holding out his hand to her.

This time there was no hesitation. She fitted into his arms as if they had been designed for her. 'This is lovely,' she murmured.

'Magic,' he replied.

Magic, she thought. That was just the word.

After a couple more dances, they went outside for another walk in the garden, but discovered with a nasty shock that everyone else seemed to have the same idea. They found the same private path as before, came to what she thought of as *their* bench—and there was a couple already sitting on it. And they were kissing! They struck off down a side path to another seat and there was another entwined couple.

'Pah! All this kissing on benches,' muttered Connor in her ear. 'We did it first. Did we start a craze or did everyone work it out for themselves?'

Zoe had been feeling hard done by, but knowing that Connor felt the same cheered her up. 'It's just a romantic night,' she told him. 'Let everybody share it.'

'I'm selfish. I don't want their romantic nights interfering with mine.' He looked down at her in the dimness. 'We are having a romantic night, aren't we?'

Zoe caught her breath. Did he mean now—or later? 'Very romantic,' she said.

They turned another corner. For the moment, there was no one in sight. Connor quickly pulled her into his arms and kissed her. It felt deliciously urgent. 'That's better,' he said. 'It'll do to be going on with.'

Did that mean what she thought it might mean? Was she going to try and fight it?

At the close of the evening the taxi dropped Jo and Sam off and took Zoe and Connor on to the coach house. 'Ouch! My feet!' said Zoe as she stepped down to the road. She hung on to Connor's arm for balance. 'I haven't danced so much for years.'

'But did you enjoy it?'

'Tremendously. You?'

'More than any night I can remember,' said Connor. 'Ever.'

# CHAPTER NINE

AND now Zoe was on the patio of her home and alone with Connor. The happy, joking mood that had been so obvious when there were four of them had disappeared. Something more serious had taken its place. 'You aren't going straight home, are you?' she said. Not a question or a challenge but a simple statement of fact.

He traced the side of her face with his hand. 'No.'

The intensity of that one word took her breath away. She moistened her lips. 'Would you like a drink?'

'Tea,' he said. 'Champagne is all very well, but now I'm thirsty.'

She smiled. 'Me too. Tea it shall be.' She looked at him, his dinner jacket slightly rumpled, his beautiful shirt not quite so pristine, his tie loosened. It was difficult to imagine how much more gorgeous he could look. 'It's a warm night. Why don't you take off your jacket and tie?'

'I thought you'd never ask.'

Oops, were things moving a bit fast? 'The sunset's long gone, I'm afraid,' she said quickly, 'but sit down anyway. I'll be right with you.' She wasn't avoiding what might be coming. Rather, she was putting off the moment, giving herself time, drawing out the delicious anticipation. And…all right, admit it. She was just a bit afraid.

She filled the kettle and then hurried upstairs. She had felt glamorous and magical in her new dress, but now the evening was taking a different course and she needed to be able to relax. It only took a minute for her to slide the dress over her head, hang it in the wardrobe and pull on a sleeveless silk wraparound shift. Before going downstairs she changed a couple of things in her bedroom—just in case.

He patted the bench next to him as she carried a tray out to the patio, indicating that she should sit next to him, not on one of the chairs. 'You've changed your dress. You still look gorgeous.'

'Thank you, kind sir. And you look gorgeous too.'

He put his arm round her, pulled her to him and kissed her.

'That was lovely,' she whispered as it ended.

'Very lovely,' he agreed.

They reached for their tea together and for a few minutes sat companionably sipping. But there was a whole lot unsaid between them and when Zoe put her empty mug on the table and he—after a tiny hesitation—did the same, she realised it was time. The entire evening had been leading up to what might happen now. Coming this far had been a set of small conscious decisions—this was the last chance she had of changing her mind. She was going against everything she'd vowed over the past few months; she was putting her emotional self at the mercy of a man—one she had only known for a comparatively short while. And this was not something minor. She didn't do casual affairs; she never had. If she went ahead it would change her life here in Buckley for ever.

He put his hand over hers. Uncannily, he seemed to know exactly what she was feeling. 'Sweetheart, I'm uncertain too, but I think it will be all right,' he said. 'You're worried. That's understandable, but I promise the last thing in the world I want to do is hurt you. Why don't we just sit here a while longer and kiss each other some more and we'll see where things go?' He put his arm round her, close enough for her to feel reassured, loose enough that she didn't feel threatened.

And suddenly and absolutely, the magic came back and she did know. This was what she wanted. 'Kiss me again,' she said.

He kissed her. A gentle soft kiss at first, on the lips but then on her cheek, on her forehead, even on her nose. Playful kissing. A good way to start. Then he slipped his hand inside the loose front of her wraparound shift, stroked the softness of the naked flesh below. She felt his hand pause, almost as if waiting for permission to continue. For answer, she pulled him closer, heard the soft sound of pleasure deep in his throat.

'A patio bench is all right for kissing,' he murmured, 'but it can get a bit restrictive.'

There was no need for a reply. She took his hand, led him indoors and up the stairs.

When she had taken off her dress she had lit four large candles and set them on her dressing table. Now the white walls of her bedroom were illuminated by a soft, flickering yellow light. The double bed had fresh pale blue cotton sheets. The wooden furniture glimmered. The effect was warm and inviting.

He smiled with appreciation, then turned to look at her with a passion that stirred her soul. She realised that the feelings she aroused in this man were the same as those he aroused in her. But he did something that surprised her and heightened those feelings even more. He lifted her hands to his lips and kissed each one in turn. It was an unspoken statement. He would be gentle with her. She could trust him.

She stood motionless as he undid the tie of her shift, slipped it from her shoulders and let it fall in a shimmering heap round her ankles. She had on a white lacy bra and matching briefs, both bought earlier in the week because a gorgeous new dress deserved gorgeous new lingerie. She felt him drag in a breath of excitement and wonderment. 'You are so lovely,' he breathed, 'so very, very lovely.'

His kiss was deeper now and, as he pulled her closer to him, she could sense his pleasure in the contact, feel the hardness of his body. And her own body was responding. It seemed as if her bones were liquid, warmth was growing and spreading from the very centre of her. There was the strongest urge to join with him that she had ever experienced. Her body wanted both to give and to take.

He lifted his mouth from hers; for a moment she could look in his eyes. The eyes, the guardian of the soul—they told her so much. She'd seen something in them all evening and hadn't dared give it a name. But there it was. Connor cared for her; she could tell it by the way he was looking at her. That knowledge filled her with a joy that was like nothing she had felt for any man before.

He released her slowly, cupped her face in his hands and stroked his fingertips down her cheeks, across her shoulders, the swell of her breasts. Then he reached behind her, undid the clasp of her bra and slid it from her arms. She caught her breath at first, but then smiled. It was her body; she could do what she wished with it. Or let him do what he wished!

He bent his head, in turn took the pinkness of each nipple in his mouth, and she shuddered with delight as he held them, so tenderly, with his teeth. Then there was the roughness of his tongue and she pulled his body closer to hers.

Something wasn't quite right. 'You've still got your clothes on,' she said huskily. 'I want you like me.'

One more time he kissed her before lowering her onto her bed. She watched as he swiftly divested himself of his clothing. His body was as magnificent as she'd expected. Another time she'd take off his clothes for him, slowly and teasingly… Then a thought struck her. 'Connor! We have to…'

'All taken care of, sweetheart. Not that I was presuming, but…'

But he'd slipped a packet of condoms into his suit pocket

for much the same reason that she'd polished her bedroom furniture. Just because. Just in case. Because, if something wonderful *was* to happen tonight, neither of them had wanted to spoil it. The thought melted her, made her feel wanton. She lay back again, eyes half-closed, her hands clasped behind her head in a pose of suggestion, of offering.

She felt the bed dip as he knelt astride her. Their bodies weren't touching—yet—but it seemed to Zoe as if the warmth of him seeped down to cover her. He kissed her. She reached up to hold him, to pull him to her, but gently he took her arms and placed them back behind her head. 'Let me love you,' he whispered.

He kissed her face, trailed kisses down her neck, kissed her breasts again so that her nipples stood almost painfully erect. And then his head moved further down her body—what was he going to do? Surely he wasn't going to? So soon? Or was it soon? She'd lost all track of time. His fingers slid under the elastic of her briefs; instinctively she raised her hips so he could ease them down.

Now she was completely naked. Vulnerable, yet trusting. She felt her heart thudding, her breath sobbing in her throat. She was on fire with anticipation, she felt that this was what she had been born for, this was her destiny and she… 'Connor, oh, Connor!' She cried his name aloud as his head dipped between her legs, as he kissed her in that most intimate of caresses.

It was wonderful. She arched towards him, her body one great pleasure centre, waves of delight pulsing through her body. But then she realised that there were two of them and that she wanted them to be completely joined.

She reached down, felt for his shoulders. 'Connor, that's enough…you'll take me too far… I want you to…I want us to…'

He knew what she wanted, what she needed. 'I like giving you pleasure,' he said.

'I want a different pleasure now. Love me, Connor. Please?'

And then he was above her again. She knew what was to happen, but for a moment there was just glorious anticipation. She knew, after this, things would never be the same between them again. So it should be.

He was still poised, either having those same thoughts himself or simply giving her a moment to breathe normally again, letting her move back from tumbling down the edge of that wonderful precipice. She reached down between their bodies and grasped his hardness. Her hand trembled as she heard and felt his gasp of excitement.

'Now, Connor. I'm ready now!' She couldn't wait any longer. She wanted things to be brought to their natural climax. He lowered himself onto her, into her, and she sighed with delight.

He started slowly, gently, but both of them were too aroused to linger. Zoe responded to his rhythm, moved with him through pulse after pulse of delirious excitement until her cry joined with his as they reached the peak of joint ecstasy.

'That was so good. So, so good,' he said, holding her closely as their heart rates subsided and their breathing returned to normal. He kissed her hair, moved on to her face, stopped in surprise. 'Tears? Are you crying? Did I hurt you?'

'I'm crying because I'm happy,' she said. 'Now I want to go to sleep in your arms.'

But he was the one who slept first. She lay next to him, his arms round her, listening to his breathing, feeling the warmth of his breath on her face.

She was happy, drowsy and utterly relaxed—but also confused. What she had just shared with Connor was far more earth-shaking than anything she had experienced with Neil. Did that mean life with him might be better too? A hard core of anxiety told her that at some time over the past few weeks she'd fallen in love with Connor without realising. Had she said that tonight? She didn't think so—lovemaking was something you did with bodies, with souls, not with words.

Did it matter? Should she have said she loved him? She didn't know. After all, he hadn't said that he loved her either.

Still puzzling, not sure whether she should be exhilarated by her realisation or apprehensive, Zoe surrendered to sleep.

She woke early as usual. For a moment, feeling a warm body beside her, Zoe froze in panic. Then memory flooded back. She raised herself on one elbow, smiled down at Connor's gorgeous face on the pillow and gave him the gentlest of kisses. What would today bring? Last night had been sheer magic. Today their lives must revert to normal—but with changes. They would have to talk things over before she collected Jamie. How were they to organise their lives now? She thought it might be fun deciding.

She slipped carefully out of bed, taking care not to wake him. She went downstairs to make…What should she make? She didn't know if Connor preferred tea or coffee in the morning. He'd wanted tea last night. She made tea, hoping their habits were the same.

He hadn't moved when she tiptoed back into the bedroom. She put his mug on the table by his side of the bed, crept to her side and slipped back between the sheets without disturbing him. Or so she thought. Suddenly an arm was round her waist, she was pulled close to a hard naked body. 'You're awake,' she gasped.

He slid strong arms around her. 'I'm awake. I woke up and you weren't here and I remembered last night and thought of a whole lot more things that I wanted to do. Now you're back, I'm going to make up for lost time.' Then he kissed her.

'Things we want to do,' she mused after kissing him thoroughly back. 'It's funny you should say that. I've got a list. First of all, I'd like to lie here in your arms some more. Then there was something I meant to do last night and I didn't get the chance.'

'Oh? What was that?'

She smiled. 'Just lie on your back like I did yesterday, you know, with your hands behind your head.'

'So you can…'

'Wait and see. You are quite warm? I'm going to throw the bedclothes off.'

Now it was light she could see more of his body. It was perfection—muscled, no hint of fat, and skin like warmed silk. She bent over him, let her breasts trail across his face, then moved so they touched his chest, his abdomen even…then she took him in her mouth and revelled at the gasp of excitement that he gave.

She loved that she was giving him so much pleasure, but she was arousing him faster than he wanted. 'My turn to stop you,' he murmured, reaching to pull her up until they were level again.

He kissed her slowly, languorously, building up the passion caress by caress. Last night had been swift and almost frantic, a coming together of two people who simply could not wait. But now they had more time, they could explore each other's bodies, find out what the other liked, where to stroke, where to kiss, where even to leave the slightest suggestion of a bite. And all the time there was the delicious expectation of the ecstasy to come. By the time they finally got there, Zoe's skin was so sensitised that Connor's lightest touch was enough to send shivers rippling across her. And from the way he shouted in exultation at the finish and then buried himself in spent triumph against her she thought he too had had an experience beyond compare.

'I love you,' she whispered silently, not quite daring to say the words aloud.

Then they curled up in contented satiation—it was almost as precious a state as the act itself.

Connor opened his eyes for the second time that morning onto the square of light coming through the rose-strewn curtains of the coach house main bedroom. This time, however, Zoe was in his arms, her curves fitting beautifully into him and her hair drifting across his skin.

His hold tightened, and her eyelids fluttered open. Connor's heart thumped. She was just so gorgeous. Had he—against all expectation—found a woman who was not only generous and giving, but also wouldn't let him down? The thought made his emotions shy away.

'I never drank my tea,' he said. 'After you went to all that trouble to get up early and make it.'

'I didn't drink mine either. This man stopped me,' she told him, laughing.

'That's terrible. You can't trust anyone. Now don't argue, just lie there and I'll fetch some more.'

'All right. Oh, do you prefer tea or coffee first thing?'

'Tea,' he said, surprised. 'Why?'

She gave a tiny smile. 'No reason.'

When he got back he paused, noticing the little Regency table under the window. Zoe had made a feature of it, put a pretty lace mat and a small jug of flowers on it. He hadn't seen it last night.

She smiled when she saw where he was looking. 'Pretty, isn't it? Far too delicate to leave downstairs with Jamie charging all over the place, but it goes beautifully up here.'

He'd had her all wrong, misjudged her right from the beginning. He couldn't begin to describe the wonderful feeling that gave him.

It was gorgeous just to lie here next to Zoe, getting to know her on a physical level, both of them holding each other, stroking whichever bit of the other's naked body was handiest. He'd forgotten how lazily pleasurable such mornings could be. But Connor was conscious that time was passing. They had lives to lead outside this bed. Before last night he'd thought he'd known what his life was going to hold. But now things had changed, he wasn't sure about what was to come. He hoped he was going to like finding out.

'I've got to fetch Jamie in an hour,' she said, echoing his thoughts. She looked at him, her eyes as honest as always. 'Do you want to have coffee and scones on the patio and we can…think about things?'

He nibbled her shoulder. 'Can't we stay in bed and think? I like it here.'

'I doubt we can. Stay in bed and think, that is. To plan any kind of future, I think I need to get out in the fresh air, to have a clear head. This bedroom is full of you and me and magic. But Cinderella is back with the ugly sisters now. You know it really.'

Then she paused. 'We do have a future, don't we, Connor?'

'Last night's magic will never go,' he said, 'and I want the future to be magic too.'

She kissed him. 'Come on, you. Time to get up.'

He knew she was right, but he'd been without this particular sort of magic for such a long time that he wanted it to continue, even for a little while.

But she rolled out of bed away from him and headed for the shower. 'You've got five more minutes to laze,' she called. 'Then you can have the bathroom while I make elevenses.'

On the patio, he thought glumly. Where they would have to be grown-up again.

Of course he had nothing to change into so he came down in his dress trousers and open-necked white shirt. Zoe, by contrast, was in T-shirt and shorts. It made him feel self-conscious.

'The outfit still suits you,' she said, a twinkle in her eye.

'It's a good thing the neighbours aren't in to see me wearing it.'

'I'll have you know my neighbour was out all night long himself.'

He took the coffee she handed him and bit into a buttered

scone. 'Thanks.' Then a deep breath. 'Do we have to talk, Zoe? Can't we just be?'

She sat down abruptly. 'Part of me wants to. But most of me wants to know where we stand.' She twisted her hands together. 'This is really hard for me, Connor. I promised myself that I'd stay man-free for Jamie's sake. I'm not having anyone else compromising his happiness. I also decided it for my own sake. Neil hurt me very badly and I didn't want to be hurt again. I thought I'd accepted that, within myself. I thought I'd settled for not sharing my life with anyone. But you aren't just anyone. I've fallen in love with you. And now I don't know what to do.'

She loved him. He was suffused with an immense joy. And also awe, because when Zoe loved she did it wholeheartedly, no matter how unworthy the loved one. 'I would never put Jamie at risk,' he said.

She gave a shaky laugh. 'Or, at least, not without training him for it first. There are other ways of hurting a child. Playing with him one day and ignoring him the next. Breaking promises. Forgetting to pick him up. Creating such a reputation for yourself that people talk and your child suffers by implication. People change and I was wrong before. I love you, but Connor, I'm so scared—how can I risk it again?'

Tears were trickling down her cheeks. Why was she sitting in a chair instead of on the bench where he could put his arm around her? 'Zoe,' he said urgently. 'Zoe, that part of your life is over. I'm not Neil; I'm me, Connor. And I want to make you and Jamie happy. And that's all I need to make me happy. Now come and sit here by me. I need my arm round you; just touching you gives me so much pleasure.'

So she sat beside him on the bench and he put his arm round her shoulders and kissed her. 'I didn't say it, did I?' he asked. 'It was something I thought I'd never say again. But I love you too.'

'We love each other. That's all that's needed; nothing can go wrong.' She laughed softly. 'And we've both fought so hard against any kind of commitment. But there was no chance. Right from the start—remember that spark?'

'I remember. Then we tried to be just friends and that didn't work either.'

'True.' She slipped her arm round his waist, rested her head on him. 'It'll all be different now.'

'I still don't know you very well,' he said after a few minutes' silent bliss. 'Now I want to know everything. What were you like as a child? You've told me about wanting to be a midwife and having trouble with your mother. But what about the real you? What were your dreams?'

'You know about the midwife dream,' she said sleepily. 'Other than that, I was just the same as any other young girl. I'd daydream and call it planning. I wanted a husband and family. A real family. All I really wanted was for my kids to have the brothers and sisters that I hadn't had. I picked three boys' names and three girls' names, just to be safe. Ideally, I wanted a mixture, but I'd be happy whatever I had. And of course I kept on changing my choices.'

'You wanted three children?'

She heard the reserve in his voice, felt him stiffen against her, and realised with alarm what she had said and how he might interpret it. 'That was when I was young, Connor! I knew nothing about motherhood then. I'm perfectly happy with just Jamie—and now I've got you and that's wonderful.'

'But you said you wanted three children. Why change your mind?'

She had been so happy. But now, hearing his carefully controlled question, suddenly she felt she was on the edge of a precipice, a chasm in front of her and there was no way she could stop herself falling. 'It doesn't matter! I've got Jamie and I'm perfectly happy. No, it's more than that; we've got

Jamie together. You must realise that he has come to see you as a father. All that talk of three; it was just what I dreamed as a young girl.'

There was an infinity of desolation in his voice. 'Funny, we're alike. I wanted three children too, but I'd only picked two names. I thought that would be enough to start with. Don't laugh; one of the names was James.'

'Connor, I'm not laughing. I think…I think the coincidence is wonderful. You've got your James.'

He shook his head slowly. 'You're still young, Zoe. I think you're over Neil now. At the moment you're happy, but eventually you'll ache for more children.'

Zoe knew where he was heading, was desperate to stop him going further. 'Connor, all I want is you and Jamie! That's all I need to make me happy!'

She thought she had never heard such misery in a voice. 'But I can't give you children. I'm infertile. Sterile.' The words felt as if they were being ripped out of him, leaving behind a gaping wound which would never heal. He loved Zoe more than anything, but what she'd told him confirmed every doubt he'd ever harboured—he couldn't give her everything she most wanted, and she deserved a man who could make her every wish come true.

'I know! I don't care! But if it bothers *you,* just think what the future might bring. There are experiments with stem cells. There's that one in a million chance. There's always hope. Or we could adopt if you're desperate for a bigger family. Connor, you're a born father; it's what you are supposed to be.' Zoe gasped for breath, trying to choke back tears. How could things change so quickly from happiness to despair?

'And you're a born mother, Zoe. It's what you are supposed to be. You need, you deserve, to have more children.' His voice grew harsher. 'Tell me what it was like, what you felt when you had Jamie. Tell me!'

She knew that this was the last thing she ought to say but there could be no lying to him. 'It was…it was the most magic moment of my life. But that doesn't matter! Connor, last night was magic and we both felt it. You know that. Connor, don't throw what we've found away!'

He stood, his face ashen. 'This is the hardest thing I've ever had to do in my life. But we both know this is the right thing to do.'

'No, we don't know,' she cried. Why wouldn't he listen? Was he so traumatised by his own tragedy that he couldn't believe her love for him overrode it all? 'We don't know that at all!'

But he was inexorable. 'What we had last night I'll remember till the day I die. It wasn't casual, it wasn't an affair; it was lovemaking in every sense of the word. I love you so much, Zoe, but that's why we have to part. I love you too much to tie you down.'

He was going! She cast around in desperation for something to say to make him see his mistake, to stop him from walking away and destroying all her new and fragile hopes and dreams for them both. 'What about Jamie? You're not just hurting me. You'll be hurting him!'

She saw his face twist with even more grief. 'I know. I only hope that my decision will ultimately be the best for him.'

'You hope? You have no idea! So what do we do now?'

He shook his head. 'I don't know. I don't want to make your life harder than necessary. Maybe I should leave the practice. Sell up. Start over.'

At those words all her hope, all her anger drained away. He was a good doctor, he belonged here, but his stupid, noble misery was about to encase him in ice all over again. She couldn't bear it. 'There's no need for that,' she said quietly. 'I can cope—and Jamie will have to. Connor, I love you—infertile or not—but you've made your mind up and there doesn't seem to be anything I can say to change it. I have to ask you one thing, though, for Jamie's sake, not mine. Don't simply stop seeing him. You needn't spend as much time with him as you have been doing, if you don't want to. Maybe tail it off gradually. He's still unsure after coming up here. You've been his cure, you know that. Just another month? Perhaps two?'

'That's fair. I...I shall miss him, Zoe.'

She couldn't help herself. 'And me? Will you miss me?'

His face betrayed his pain. 'Yes, you know I will. Zoe, you can't hate me any more than I hate myself. But I can't give you what you need. One day you'll thank me for this.'

That idea was so ludicrous that she couldn't even summon up the energy to reply.

He was silent a moment and then said, 'So what about us? If I'm to stay here and not sell up? How will we manage?'

'By seeing as little of each other as possible,' she said bitterly. 'And when we do meet—why, we'll just pretend.'

'Just pretend,' he repeated. 'Right.'

He turned and walked down the path. And, as she watched him go, taking her heart and her dreams with him, the tears she'd been holding back finally fell.

# CHAPTER TEN

LIFE had to go on—even if it seemed unendurable. Zoe drove to Jo's house to pick up Jamie. She parked outside, heard the noise of children playing and peered over the hedge. Her heart turned over when she saw a laughing Jamie being chased across the lawn by Jo's two girls. And Jo supervising, reclining in a deckchair, straw hat on head, a book in her hand. Everyone was so happy! Why couldn't she be happy too, instead of feeling completely emotionally devastated?

She pushed open the garden gate, walked across the lawn. 'Mummy!' A little body hurtled towards her, arms outstretched. She picked him up, hugged him, tears misting her vision. It was good to know that somebody loved her.

She kissed him, put him down and managed to say, 'I'll be with you in a minute, sweetheart. Just going to talk to Auntie Jo.' And Jamie ran off.

Jo looked up as she saw her friend walking towards her. Then she saw Zoe's face and her smile faded. 'Zoe, what is it? You look terrible; what's happened to you?'

Too much concern, too much kindness. Zoe found she couldn't speak. She stood there, desolate, face tear-streaked, and shook her head.

'Inside. The kids will be all right on their own. I know just the thing you need.' Jo seized her arm, pulled her indoors and guided her to an armchair. 'Sit there, close your eyes, try to relax and we'll talk in a minute. But first…'

Zoe tried to do as she was told. After a moment she felt a glass being pushed into her hand. 'Just sip that.'

She did. Then she coughed, spluttered, coughed again. Neat brandy! She rarely drank neat spirits. And never in the middle of the day. But the fiery liquid did something for her, jerked her out of her shock.

'Finish it, and then we'll have some tea and you can tell me what's wrong,' Jo said.

So Zoe finished the drink and felt—not better, but less worse. At least she was able to talk. 'Connor and I spent the night together,' she said, 'and it was miraculous. Then this morning…this morning when I thought I couldn't be any happier, we talked about having children. Jo, this is his secret but you're my best friend and…well, because of having Lyme disease, he can't now have children. So he's gone all stubborn and noble and *stupid* and thinks he mustn't come near me.'

'Oh, honey!' Jo hugged her sympathetically. 'Men! God's gift to themselves. Didn't you tell him you didn't mind?'

'Well, of course I did! But he's quite sure he knows what's best for me. Jo, what am I going to do?'

'I don't know what you're going to do in the long term, but I know what you're going to do right now. Jamie's happy playing. Sam's at the surgery doing paperwork. You are going upstairs to sleep for a couple of hours. Emotion is more tiring than hard work.'

'I couldn't sleep!'

'Try it and find out.'

So Zoe did. And, to her amazement—she slept.

She was dreading going home, to the place where she had been rejected with such shocking suddenness, but she knew it had to be faced. She had come to love her little coach house. It felt more of a home than ever the London flat had. Always, in the past few months, no matter how enjoyable the day had been, she had been glad to enter the front door. Now she wondered if she'd ever sit on the patio again and not think of this morning's heartbreak.

There was a note pushed through the letter box. She recognised Connor's bold handwriting, and her heart leaped.

*Zoe—Just to let you know that I will be away all next week. I found a cancellation on a course for new drugs use for GPs and Sam agrees that it would be a good idea if I went on it. Back next weekend. Tell Jamie we'll play football when I get back. I'm sorry—Connor.*

Zoe blinked back tears. Just for a moment she'd thought he might have changed his mind. She looked at the note again. *Away all next week.* It was probably for the best. It would give her some time to subdue these new longings in her heart, to work out if they really could coexist without her wanting to be with him. To start all over again with this fresh life of hers.

She told Jamie that Uncle Connor would be away for a few days, but that he could go still into the big garden as long as she was with him.

Jamie was tired and didn't need much reading when he was put to bed. Once he was asleep, Zoe stood at her window looking across at Connor's house. All the windows were dark. She felt unbearably lonely. She hadn't realised just how much she'd been comforted by the knowledge that Connor was so close.

Going to bed was worse. She had her usual bath, slid between the sheets wanting only the oblivion of sleep—and there, just faintly, was Connor's smell. Part cologne, part masculinity. She couldn't stand it. She got up and changed the linen and pillowcases. Then climbed back into bed and sobbed her heart out.

By the end of the week she had almost accepted the awkwardness of the situation. She talked to Jo, said she had thought of leaving, but it was difficult because she and Jamie were so happy here.

'You've made a home in Buckley, that's why,' said Jo. 'It suits you and you suit it. It's a daft idea to leave.' She shook her head crossly. 'I don't know whether to shake Connor or applaud him! I think he's wrong in what he's done but I can almost admire his strength in doing what he said. Because I do think he loves you. It was fairly obvious from the way he was looking at you at the ball.'

'That only makes things worse,' Zoe said flatly.

He came back to work the following week. She saw his lights on Sunday night, knew they had to meet and had been preparing herself. The first time she saw him in the corridor, she put a false smile on her face. 'Hi, welcome back. People have been asking after you. Was it a good course?'

He looked almost shocked at her cheerful facade. Then assumed his courteous, slightly distant manner. 'Yes, the course was very interesting. I learned a lot. Has everything been…okay while I was away?'

'Jamie missed you, but he played in your garden. He'll be glad to see you.' She moistened her lips, but carried on. 'There's been a bit of speculation by people who were at the ball and thought they'd seen more than really existed. All died down now.'

He closed his eyes briefly, as if in pain. 'That's something, I suppose. And you?'

'Fine.'

'Good.' He didn't seem very convinced. Was he finding this

as difficult as she was? People passing in the corridor must think that they were just a couple of colleagues, having a chat. They couldn't feel the hidden messages passing from one to the other.

'I've bought Jamie a small present,' he said. 'A new football.'

'That's nice of you. I'll send him over this evening. But don't let him interfere with your life.'

Connor winced at this and she felt slightly guilty.

'I'll try not to,' he said.

Jamie ran straight over after school, returning after a while, happy with his new football but saying that Uncle Connor had to work hard to catch up after being away. 'He said he might see me tomorrow,' he added.

This is how it's going to be, thought Zoe. But I can cope. I have to.

But coping was all it was. It was as if she'd been so piercingly happy for that short time when she knew she loved Connor and knew her loved her that now there was no middle path for her to take. She was worried that Jamie might suffer, but fortunately he started getting excited about Sports Day, staying after school twice a week to practice for it. She hoped it might make up for him not seeing quite so much of Connor. It was just a pity she couldn't find a similar remedy for herself.

And then, after a dreadful day of home visits and hospital trips, Connor came to her door. The first time since they had parted. He caught her with a trayful of newly baked scones—just as he had that very first time. As she heard the click of the gate and looked up to see him walking through her garden, her memories of that occasion came flooding back. How things had changed.

He looked almost as ill at ease as she was. 'Hi.'

Love, misery and a desperate need to appear calm coursed through her. 'Hi. How are you?'

'Fine. Look, I don't want to disturb you. I've got to get back for evening surgery, but…'

'You're not disturbing me. And evening surgery isn't for ages yet. Connor, we're managing at work. We can still be polite to each other at home, can't we?'

There was a tiny pause. 'Of course.'

*Still be polite to each other.* Even as she spoke the words, she knew they were ridiculous. What they had shared went far beyond simple politeness. She bit her lip. 'So why are you here?'

'Jamie was saying it's his birthday soon. Apparently being six is the greatest age ever because it means he can join the school football team next year.'

'So I've been told. Frequently.' This was awful. She gripped the tray of scones, unable to think what to do with it. 'Do you want a scone?' she asked.

It obviously wasn't something that he had expected. 'Well, yes, but…'

'Go and sit on the patio. I'll bring some out.' And if sitting on the patio brought back memories that were uncomfortable, well, that was too bad. She turned her back on him, assembling a tray, putting the kettle on too to give herself time. He took the hint and retreated.

'Right, Jamie's birthday,' she said brightly when she joined him. 'It's in a fortnight. I've promised him a party. It'll mean quite a few shouting children, I'm afraid. I'll try and keep the noise down, obviously.'

Connor had turned his scone over and was smiling at the face underneath. Quite a bleak smile, but it almost unmanned Zoe to see it.

'You know perfectly well he's welcome to bring his friends into my garden, noisy or not, and I'll be upset if he doesn't!'

He means it, she realised, as she looked at his fierce expression—and had to concentrate hard not to weep for the unfairness of life. 'That's very kind of you,' she said.

'It'll give me pleasure. Zoe, that's not what I came across for. You know it's Buckley Show this weekend?'

'I can hardly miss it; the posters are everywhere!'

'Of course they are. The local agricultural show is a big occasion.'

'I've never been to one before. Jo and Sam and the family are going on the Sunday. I expect Jamie and I will go with them. I gather there's a small funfair with roundabouts and so on, as well as a show ring and a competition marquee.'

'Yes, all of that,' said Connor. He looked more uncomfortable than Zoe had ever seen him. 'And more, too. Zoe, there's something I think Jamie will really like. Something I arranged before…before…'

'Before you decided you couldn't have a relationship with me after all because you couldn't father children? Totally ignoring what I felt about it? And just after you had spent the night making love to me?'

'That isn't fair! Is that what you think of me? That I would take you to bed and then…and then…'

She had never seen him look so horrified and disgusted. 'No,' she said. 'No, I don't really think that. To tell you the truth, I'm not thinking very straight at all right at the moment.' She took a ragged breath. 'Why don't you just tell me whatever it is you arranged when we were still simply friends?'

She saw he was having difficulty in talking. She knew her words had hurt him, but he had hurt her too.

But he started, 'On Saturday, there is going to be a parade of tractors around the show ring. And a farmer patient of mine called Bert Ramsdale is taking part.'

'So?'

'Bert has the biggest, reddest tractor you have ever seen, just like in that blessed story Jamie likes so much. Anyway, some time ago I asked him—if you agree—Jamie can ride on the tractor with Bert during the parade.'

Her heart ached at the thoughtfulness of the gesture. 'A ride on a big red tractor! Connor, he'd be so excited! That's wonderful! Are you sure it's all right?'

'Bert's got grandchildren of his own, though they've grown up a bit now. He'd love to give Jamie a ride. Call it an early birthday present.'

'Oh, Connor, thank you.' She picked her next words carefully. 'What time do you want to pick him up?'

He didn't pretend to misunderstand her. 'Thank you for trusting me with him—and I'd be very happy to take him on my own. But I've just been talking to him about the fair and he's desperate to go. To go with you.' Connor looked a little shamefaced. 'He asked if I would come too. I said I'd see what work I had. And then I felt really dreadful as his little face fell. Zoe, I truly think Jamie would have a better time if all three of us went together.'

The silence between them seemed to lengthen and lengthen. The worst of it was; she knew Connor was right. And Jamie was her son and she loved him. What was one more day of pain compared to his happiness? 'All right,' she said. 'I'll come too. Like I said before, we can pretend.'

He looked relieved. 'You're very generous.'

She made a helpless gesture. 'It was nice of you to think of it in the first place.' Then compressed her lips. It hadn't been nice; it had been lovely. It had been exactly the sort of splendiferous treat a loving father would dream up for his son. *Don't go there, Zoe. Just don't go there.*

Connor stood. 'I'll come over about ten. We can walk. It'll be impossible to park.' And he was gone.

It rained during the week, curtailing Jamie's playing in Connor's garden, but Friday was drier and Saturday dawned fine and warm. Zoe took a chance on the weather and wore a pink dress that she knew flattered her and brought out the tone of her skin. It was mildly revealing too, cut low in the front. She had her pride; she wasn't going to make a fool of herself ever again, but there was no harm in reminding Connor of what he had turned down.

The dress had the desired effect. She knew him now; he couldn't conceal from her the flicker of interest when she opened the door. He was looking pretty good himself in chinos and a softly draping shirt. Had he done it on purpose? But neither of them said anything.

Jamie held a hand of each of them as they walked through the town to the big field that served as cattle market and fairground. It twisted Zoe's heart to see him so happy with both her and Connor, to see his sunny face turning from one to the other. As they approached they could hear the music coming from the PA system and Jamie jumped with joy. But Zoe had a sudden stab of memory.

'What's the matter?' said Connor.

For a moment she was furious with him. How had he known? If they were so attuned to each other, why couldn't he just trust her to know what she wanted from life? 'Nothing,' she said. 'It's silly. There used to be a big fair that set up near the army base every year in the last place we lived. Girls at school raved about how much fun it was. My mother said it was full of lawless travellers and got really distressed when I suggested that I go with a group of friends— even just for an hour. She wanted me near, all the time, wanted to wrap me in cotton wool, for her sake as well as for mine. But I could open the windows and hear the music, like this.'

'It probably wasn't that great.'

'No, but I'd have liked to find out for myself.'

'Make your own mistakes, you mean?'

'Not actually make them—just know that the potential was there to make them if I wanted to. It's no wonder, really, that I fell for Neil. Life with him was so free.' She sighed. 'I ought to have known there'd be a catch.'

They'd entered the showground now. Booths had been set up either side of the main avenue leading to the arena. Signs pointed to the animal pens, auction sheds, agricultural equipment sales, farmer's market, craft demonstrations and funfair. The place was thronged with people, queues building up already at the hot-food stalls. Jamie's eyes were out on stalks, not knowing which way to look first. Certainly he wasn't paying any attention to the adults' conversation.

'Is there always a catch?' said Connor. His voice was noncommittal, but Zoe could hear the edge to his question.

'There always has been so far,' she said frankly. 'I was glad to help my mother, but I missed out on normal growing-up, and didn't realise until later that I'd been emotionally stifled. Neil showed me bright lights and glitter—and I was so dazzled that I didn't notice there was nothing behind them. Jamie is a wonderful gift, but I have to be so responsible all the time that sometimes I forget to enjoy him.' She took a resolute breath. 'And then I find a man I love and I get hurt again.' For a moment she saw her own pain reflected in Connor's navy-blue eyes. 'Sorry. Saying that was ill-mannered of me. It won't happen again.'

'Mummy!' gasped Jamie, seeing two children run past with huge mounds of candyfloss on sticks.

Connor gave a strained chuckle. 'Later, lad. No point *starting* the day feeling sticky and sick.' He glanced at Zoe, half-angry, as if he didn't want to keep being reminded. 'I'm sorry too. But I refuse to be the means of stopping you from having a happy and fulfilled life. Look, for now let's just make Jamie's first Buckley Show a good one. Enjoy today. Time out. Pax?'

*Enjoy today.* But look what had happened the last time

they'd taken time out of their ordinary lives. She gave a sound-less sigh. 'Pax,' she agreed.

So they strolled towards the animal pens, past demonstrations of basket- weaving and hurdle-making and then to the funfair.

'Look, Jamie, lots of people going round in big teacups,' Connor said, pointing to a roundabout. 'Would you like a ride in one?'

'Yes, please,' said Jamie. 'I'd like a ride in a cup with you and Mummy. And then can I go on that big slidey thing?'

The helter-skelter. Zoe looked at the height and bit her lip. 'I'll go up with him,' said Connor. 'I'd like to.'

So Jamie had a fairing. He had rides on assorted merry-go-rounds. He won a purple helium-filled balloon with *Buckley Show* written on it. The three of them ate locally produced beefburgers and bought an ice cream each. Almost, Zoe couldn't help feeling with a pang, almost as if they had been a real family.

Then came the important bit—Jamie's early birthday present. The tractor parade! They met a smiling Bert Ramsdale and one of his grown-up grandsons, Adam, outside the main arena. Zoe liked both of them at once—more importantly, so did Jamie. In fact, Jamie was astounded. Bert was big, well-rounded, had a red face and was wearing his Farmers' Best—tweed jacket, yellow waistcoat, leather gaiters and a flat cap.

'He looks just like Farmer Giles in the *Big Red Tractor* story,' Jamie whispered.

'He does,' Zoe whispered back, 'but his name is Bert.'

'So this is my new driver, is it?' Bert said. 'Jamie, you can come and work on my farm any time.'

The arena was the main show ground where the gymkhanas, dog show and sheep-herding trials were held. Tomorrow there would be a steam rally, but today local tractors were going to drive round in a parade before the rest of the show started.

Bert took them to where the tractors were lined up, led them to the biggest and the reddest. Zoe blinked when she saw its size. 'I'll get in the cab first,' said Bert, 'and then we'll lift you up.'

'I can climb,' said Jamie. 'Uncle Connor is teaching me.' And he was up the side of the tractor like an expert.

Zoe gulped. Connor put a hand on her arm. 'No cotton wool, remember?'

'It doesn't mean I have to like it,' muttered Zoe.

Adam winked as he also swung himself up. 'Mum used to say that. He's never damaged any of us, though.'

Someone shouted a command, the marshal waved and the first tractor set off into the arena. The rest followed, one after the other. Zoe watched the tractor carrying her son as it chugged around the huge ring. She was very conscious of Connor's tall frame by her side.

The big red tractor came round in front of them again. Jamie was standing between Bert's legs, his hands on the wheel, proud and terrified at once, steering on his own. He managed to wave to them and Zoe photographed him.

Two more circuits, and then the tractors thundered magnificently out to the static display area. Jamie was hopping up and down in the cab, incandescent with joy. 'Uncle Connor, Farmer Bert says you can take us to his farm one day and we can see his other tractor. Can we?'

Connor cast a helpless glance at Zoe. 'We'll see what can be arranged,' he said. 'Now, say thank you to Farmer Bert and we'll find out what else there is to see. I think I saw signs for a Robin Hood demonstration.'

'All right,' said Jamie happily. 'Thank you *very* much, Farmer Bert. And thank you, Uncle Connor. It's the best birthday present *ever*!'

Just for a moment, as Connor smiled and swung James down from the tractor to her with Bert looking benignly on in the background, Zoe felt marvellously, completely happy. The three of them together was so as it should be. But then she remembered—they weren't together, this was a pretend day, something that would soon be in the past. She bit her lip at the shaft of pain. Still, this was Jamie's day and she had to seem cheerful. Her grief she could put on hold.

Jamie decided he didn't want candyfloss; instead, he wanted a lollipop on a stick. Zoe wasn't too happy about sweets but, remembering her own misery when not allowed to go to the fair, she agreed. 'Just this once, mind! And you clean your teeth the minute we get back home.'

Jamie smiled beatifically, stuffed the lollipop in his mouth and sucked happily as he reached for Connor's hand.

Another stab of pain. Parting Jamie from Connor was going to be hard.

They walked along the edge of the display ground towards the archery targets and longbow shooting. Behind them came the sound of a tractor engine, one of the farmers heading for home. Jamie scampered to the edge of the field for a closer look and waved at the driver, who waved back.

It always happened when you least expected it.

Zoe was looking at her son and saw suddenly and horribly what was about to happen. She couldn't move, couldn't yell a warning: there was nothing she could do. Everything seemed to happen in slow motion and she was completely paralysed with terror. There was a drainage ditch to the side of the path that led from the display ground. Perhaps the rain earlier in the week had softened the bank, perhaps the bank was undercut, perhaps the weight of all the tractors during the day had softened it. Whatever…The tractor drove too close to the edge.

The ground looked solid but it wasn't. In horrific, slowed-down detail, the vast back wheel skidded, slipped, dropped into the ditch. The tractor tilted, lurched sideways, slowly toppled on its side.

And Jamie was in the way! Dear God, he was right in its

path! Zoe's heart leapt into her throat as she started to scream. She screamed as the driver's canopy pushed Jamie over. She screamed as the cab slammed into the ground. She screamed as Jamie disappeared from view.

Connor had been looking the other way but, at the roar of the tractor's engine and Zoe's scream, he turned. She caught sight of his face, saw his expression of utter horror before he was hurtling towards the tractor and she was following.

The noise of the engine stopped. The driver squirmed out of the cab, blood streaming from a cut on his head. 'I fell on the little lad,' he mumbled. 'He's under the canopy; I'll have to…'

'Go over there and sit down,' Connor snapped, barely pausing in his swift assessment of the wreckage. 'Hold a handkerchief to your head. We'll deal with this.'

Zoe was frantically scrambling up the crumbling bank, digging her fingers into the dirt to get a purchase. Connor appeared beside her, his face intent. The horror was still in his eyes, but overlaying it was the purposeful expression of a professional. She felt, not relief, but the certainty that if anything could be done then Connor could do it. In some ways the complete trust was a comfort. It meant she wasn't alone.

And then she heard a strange cry, half gasp, half cough.

'Mummy…'

Jamie was alive!

Connor gripped her arm. 'Thank God,' he whispered.

Zoe took her own tearing breath and concentrated. And had to bite her lips together not to cry aloud again. Jamie was pinned down by one of the struts that supported the driver's canopy. It was pressed across his abdomen, pushing him into the muddy ground below. His face was white, his eyes wide and fearful. She tried to reach for him, to comfort him, but Connor took a deep lungful of air and said, 'Careful. I'll see to him.'

He slid down to kneel by Jamie's side, feeling under the

strut, scooping at the oozing mud. 'He's been pushed into soft earth,' he muttered. 'There might be no internal damage if we're in luck…' Then he tensed. 'Zoe! Lean over his face, check his airway and his breathing!'

She did as she was told. There were new signs of panic in her son's eyes. His mouth opened even wider and suddenly she realised that his lips were turning blue. 'Connor! He can't breathe!'

Connor pushed her aside, bent low over Jamie, eased his head back and looked in his mouth. 'His tongue's okay… Oh, God! That lollipop he was sucking! He must have tried to swallow it in his shock, and now it's lodged in his throat!'

'Heimlich manoeuvre!' said Zoe, almost too terrified to speak.

'I can't! There's no way I can get behind him. But perhaps there's just a chance…'

He put the knuckles of his right hand under Jamie's diaphragm and jerked them sharply upwards. He tried, five times. It could work—but it didn't. Zoe found panic seizing her.

Jamie's head lolled to one side. No air to his lungs, no oxygen to his bloodstream, feeding and powering the rest of the body. Zoe was a midwife—she had seen babies who had been starved of oxygen. She knew only too well what would happen if there was insufficient oxygen reaching the brain. Brain death in three minutes.

There was a crowd gathering behind them, some to watch, some offering to help. Connor turned his head and shouted, 'I need a pocket knife! Any kind of blade! Now!'

Three were thrust forward. He grabbed one, opened the smallest blade and nodded. From his pocket he took a ballpoint pen and pulled out the ink cartridge so he was left with a hollow tube. Then he turned to her. His face was grey, his voice clipped to the point of curtness—but she knew he was in extreme stress, not unfeeling, and she loved him for it, even through her terror.

'Pull his head back, hold it straight between your hands.'

She followed his directions without question. She knew what he was doing, knew she had to do the same. For the moment, put all emotion on hold. It was the only way they could manage this—to treat it as a job. But she couldn't. This was her son. And treating him was the man she loved. There *had* to be a happy outcome. Almost unconsciously, she started crooning restful words, getting Jamie to relax, making it easier for Connor to do what he had to do.

He was feeling the strain too. She knew it. He talked as he worked, perhaps to her, perhaps to himself. 'Just below the Adam's apple there's a ridge called the cricoid cartilage. I have to put my finger on the soft spot between them. Tighten the skin over the spot and cut—about half an inch deep.'

The penknife looked clumsy in his hands—but it cut. Zoe cringed at the sight of her son's blood, but her hold didn't alter.

And nor did her faith in Connor. He was more intense than she'd ever seen him. He looked at the cut for a millisecond, slipped a finger inside to enlarge it, then slid the biro tube into the cut, put his mouth over the end—and breathed air into Jamie's lungs. After a small nightmare of black endless nothing, there came the whistling sound that indicated that Jamie was once again breathing on his own.

'Thank God,' whispered Conner. 'Oh, thank God.'

Zoe gave a small, stifled sob of relief.

Their eyes met. There was no need for words. Both knew the other was more full of emotion than they could express. And, in that moment, Zoe's feelings crystallised. She loved this man. Not because of Jamie, but because of her. She loved him. She had trusted him to save her son's life and, more than anything, she wanted to trust him with her heart. Forget pride, forget hurt, forget not laying herself on the line again. As soon as they got out of this situation, she was going to tell him that she couldn't live without him.

Connor looked back down at Jamie. Still holding the tube in place, he leaned back, a huge relieved smile on his face. 'That's better,' he said.

Ragged applause sounded behind them. Zoe gazed at Jamie, his colour normal again, and knew a vast, overwhelming thankfulness. 'What do we do now?'

'We stay right here and wait for the professionals.'

And, on cue, there was the thin sound of the siren as the paramedics drove towards them.

They sat in the corner of a waiting room in Sheffield Hospital. Zoe was leaning against Connor's shoulder; his arm was round her. From time to time she shuddered and his arm tightened.

'He'll be all right, won't he?' she whispered, not for the first time.

But, despite everything, Connor was still a doctor and would not give good news until he was absolutely sure. 'I think there's a very good chance,' he said. 'The ambulance got us here so fast it must have been jet-propelled. Try and relax.'

'Why are they taking so long?' she said fretfully.

'They're making certain. I'd do exactly the same. So would you.'

She was silent for a few moments and then she said, 'I'm glad you're with me.'

Then the A&E Consultant came out and smiled. 'Mrs Hilton? Good news. Young Jamie has a badly bruised abdomen but there appears to be no internal damage. You were right, Dr Maitland. Apparently, the soft ground saved him. No other problems, except for the dirtiest piece of surgery I've seen in a long time on his neck. An emergency tracheotomy! Penknife and ballpoint pen? I've heard of it being done but this is the first time I've ever had to deal with it. Still, a very good, efficient job. I've cleaned it all up and antibiotics will see to any risk of infection. I gather you've had some experience of surgery before?'

'Some,' said Connor.

'Rather more conventional, I trust. Now, we're going to keep Jamie in overnight for observations. Would you like to come and see him? He's only half conscious but he might recognise you.'

Zoe and Connor stood. 'Perhaps you should go in on your own,' Connor said. 'After all, he's your child.'

She took his hand in a firm hold. This was where it started. 'He's yours as well now. After all, you saved his life.' Then she turned to the doctor. 'We don't want to leave him. Is there somewhere we can stay the night? Both of us?'

'I'll arrange it,' said the doctor.

# CHAPTER ELEVEN

THEY sat on either side of Jamie's bed, each clasping one of his hands. Connor looked at Jamie, white-faced, a bandage round his neck, more or less asleep. Then he looked at Zoe, watched her gently lift her child's hand to her lips.

Today had taught him so much. He enjoyed his work, got satisfaction from mending the townsfolk in the surgery and then pushing himself in the open air on his time off, but today was the first time he had really known what his life would be like without Zoe, because he knew that if he hadn't been able to save Jamie, the Zoe he knew might not have survived. She would have continued her life as normal, but her very essence, the loving nature that so attracted him to her, would have died with her son. Before she had come to Buckley he hadn't even realised that his daily round was empty. In shutting out the pain of what could never be, he'd shut out all the ordinary stuff of life too. But she had come, with her wide smile and her refusal to take the easy path. She'd blown a hole in his armour—and when he'd finished reeling in shock he'd discovered that she and Jamie had set up home in his soul.

Now he thought of Jo and Sam and their family, he thought of Alice and Tim Reynolds and their late pregnancy, he thought of the other members of staff. For goodness' sake, he even thought of Barbara and Roy Reagan. Their life had been a bit of a mess. But it was improving; there was a genuine love for each other.

All these people had something that he didn't have—something that he wanted so desperately. But…could he be selfish enough ask Zoe to marry him? He had told her that she was a born mother, entitled to more children. Children that he couldn't give her. The memory of that day was still inky-black in his mind. He shifted in his chair, watching her. There must be no more pain today, no more anxiety. She had fixed all her attention on her child and nothing else mattered.

Then she looked up, straight into his eyes. 'Don't you dare even think of leaving,' she said.

Bright threads of heat arrowed through all his veins. 'Zoe, I…'

'I mean it!'

Hope filled him at her fierceness, impossible and overwhelming. Like it had on the day she'd taken him by the hand and led him to her bed.

'I…' He cleared his throat and tried again. 'I was thinking I'd ring Jo. If you're to stay the night you'll need clothes… stuff…' His voice trailed off.

'*We'll* need clothes and stuff,' Zoe corrected him.

So she'd meant it when she said to the doctor that they would both stay the night in the hospital to be near Jamie? Warmth flooded him anew. He shouldn't be feeling this, shouldn't be letting this wonderful well-spring of hope bubble up. He should be suppressing it, reverting to his unemotional surgeon mode. It was safer.

Safer. But also empty.

'I'll phone Jo,' he said. 'I'll find out where they're putting us. Then I'll be back.'

He walked outside, hardly noticing the curious looks that his muddy, dishevelled clothes were attracting. His mind was wholly and completely taken up with Zoe. There was no room for anything else.

Jo was worried—and angry. 'Connor, what's this about Jamie having an accident? Where's Zoe? I've been worried sick! I've had the chief marshal at the show on to me *and* the local paper wanting a statement. Why didn't you phone? Five messages I've left you! Five! What's going on?'

Connor leaned against the wall of the hospital and let Jo's voice wash over him. His stomach growled, reminding him that neither he nor Zoe had eaten for hours. He'd fix that as soon as he'd finished here. 'Sorry, Jo. Jamie had an accident at the fair and I had to do an emergency tracheotomy, but he's now okay and he's going be fine. Zoe and I are at Sheffield Hospital with him. We're going to stay the night. If you can find us some clothes and necessities…'

This was what Jo did. She sorted out situations. 'Well, of course I can,' she said crossly. 'I suppose you want your car there too, do you? Leave everything to me.'

Connor smiled. 'Thanks. We're a bit wiped out. We'll fill you in when you get here.'

There was a suspicion of a sniff. 'No need—as long as I know you're all safe. But Connor—?'

'Yes?'

'You know I never interfere with the personal lives of the people I work with?'

He had to grin. 'Like you didn't interfere with Barbara Reagan?'

'That was different. I'm just saying that if you can't see Zoe for what she is, then you're a bigger fool than I took you for.' And she rang off.

'I'm not a fool; I'm a realist,' he said to the dead phone.

He leaned against the wall for a moment longer, thinking about what he'd just said. Was he a realist or a fool? Or were all realists fools? Would it be selfish if he did what he'd known for so long he desperately wanted to do? To marry Zoe? To be a father to Jamie? Her words to him on the ward—and the warm hope inside him—suggested that was what she wanted too.

He let images of her fill his mind. Zoe, playing with Jamie. Zoe, pluckily determined on her first climb. Zoe, enraged because she thought he had endangered her child, then remorseful and ruthlessly honest when he showed her otherwise. Zoe, naked and gorgeous and laughing as they made love.

What to do?

Zoe was drowsing, lying in wonderfully warm and scented water, covered in foam, when Connor knocked on the bathroom door of the hospital flat.

'Come in,' she called, and smiled at the way he very carefully avoided looking at her as he placed the mug of tea on the end of the bath.

'I'll be out in a minute,' she said. 'It'll be wonderful to put on clean clothes. Jo is just so terrific, isn't she?'

Her friend had burst into the ward, kissed everyone in sight, sat with her arms round Zoe hearing the whole story of the day and then gone, leaving two suitcases containing enough stuff for a fortnight, let alone one evening. She'd also given Connor his car keys. But he was still here.

'She is,' he agreed. 'It's good to have friends. Good to be loved. I think I've been forgetting that.'

His eyes were on her face as he said this. Zoe tingled all over. There was a meaning there that was more than mere words. She only hoped it was the right one.

She looked at him now. He had had a bath and changed his clothes while she with Jo and was now dressed in dark trousers and a soft dark sweater. As ever, he looked good.

She drew a resolute breath. Jamie was sleeping peacefully in the ward and the Sister would send for her if there was any need. It was time to concentrate on herself, time to remake her life. And, from the expression in Connor's eyes, he might at last be ready to talk.

But, 'I've been to the hospital shop,' he said. 'Bought us some provisions. I didn't think you'd want to go back out to the café.'

'Deciding things for me again?' Her tone was wry.

'Deciding things for me,' he said. He hesitated, then leaned over the bath, put a hand on her wet, naked back and quickly kissed her. '*I* didn't want to go out to the café. And I wanted to make you a meal.'

She grinned. 'I can live with that.'

Just so long as it wasn't a goodbye gift.

Afterwards, Zoe couldn't have said what they'd eaten. All sorts of bits, washed down with a glass of wine. Her whole existence was centred on the man sitting opposite her, the man looking back at her in that half-apprehensive, half-determined way.

'Well?' she said, tense with anticipation after he'd cleared away.

He sat down again, leaned forward and took her hands. 'First I want to say sorry for the pain I've caused you.'

'Which has been great,' she put in steadily.

He bowed his head. 'Which has been great. Zoe, the accident to Jamie—things could have gone so badly wrong, and if they had I'd have lost you both. It made me think.'

'It was about time something did. Connor, didn't you ever listen to me at all? Didn't you hear me say that I don't care if we never have any children?'

'I heard, but I knew better. In some ways, I think I still do.'

But he was gripping her hands as he said it and that gave Zoe the courage to carry on. 'Wrapping me in cotton wool, in fact. Knowing what's best for me, just as everyone in my life has always done. Connor, you were the one who told me Jamie had to make his own mistakes. I'd been frightened of making another mistake myself for so long, but as soon as I did make a decision, you tried to stop me!'

'I know. I faced that this afternoon. I told you before that I loved you. I meant it. I think I always will. And when I told you I couldn't marry you because I couldn't have children, I did that for you. Or I thought I did.'

There was such misery in his voice. Zoe stood upright, pulling him to his feet. 'Hold me,' she said.

His arms came round her, giving comfort and taking it in return. 'Now I think it was cowardice on my part. You were willing to take a risk. Why wasn't I? Because I was fixated on avoiding unhappiness. And that was so wrong.'

'So?' she asked, her breath catching in her throat.

'This afternoon, I'd have done that tracheotomy on any child that had needed it. I'd have been cool, clinical, precise— the skills would have clicked into place without me even noticing.' He let go of her and cupped her face between his palms. His eyes bored into her with their intentness. 'But I wasn't cool and clinical, Zoe. The part of me that wasn't being a surgeon was terrified. You'd taught me what it is to love, what it is to feel. Jamie as well, but mostly you. That's the reason I'd have felt empty without you both. Because if you've never loved you don't know how to feel loss. You've given me that gift. You're the most wonderful thing that has ever happened to me. I love you so much, Zoe. I want to marry you and let the future take care of itself. It could be good, it could be bad, but we'll have each other. I'll be as good a father as I can to Jamie. There'll be the three of us. And I'll do everything in my power to make you happy. So will you marry me? Please, Zoe?'

Zoe gripped Connor's arms, as shaken by emotion as he was. So much in one day! The pain of being with Connor this morning had been as nothing to her fear when she'd thought Jamie might die. And then her realisation that she could trust him through thick and thin, her knowledge that she *would* try again, that she would make him see. And now happiness beyond compare, even greater than when they'd made love after the ball, because this time they'd so nearly lost it for good.

Happiness! It surrounded her, it enveloped her, it lifted her off her feet and propelled her into Connor's arms with a wordless cry. Their lips met—their tongues, mouths and hearts forever entwined. The world was encased in sunshine; the future would be magnificent…

Eventually they paused for breath. Zoe discovered that she was sitting on Connor's lap and they had somehow got into the bedroom. 'Do you really need an answer?' she asked, her heart full of joy. 'Of course I'll marry you. And I intend making you just as happy as you'll make me.'

Then she looked at the room and giggled. 'Oh, dear,' she said. 'Two single beds.'

Connor was ever practical. 'We'll push them together.' Then turned back to her with the most glorious look of love in his eyes. 'That's if I can let go of you long enough to do it.'

# EPILOGUE

SPRINGTIME. There were snowdrops in the lanes around Buckley and snowdrops spreading from the coach house garden to the play dell in Connor's garden next door.

Zoe leaned out of her bedroom window and thought dreamily that they matched the white of her dress—her wedding dress. Top Two Toe, Jo's miracle dress shop tucked away down the back street in Buckley, had done her proud. A fitted bodice that did much for her figure, and a long skirt that wasn't too long for dancing. Because Zoe and Connor would have to dance on their wedding night.

It was nine months now since Zoe had come to live in Buckley but she had made more friends here than in her whole life before. And she now had a family! 'Just you wait,' Connor had warned her with a smile. 'The minute I tell my sisters that we're getting married, we'll be invaded!' And they had been. First his sisters, their husbands and families had arrived to briefly fill Connor's big house and make themselves known to Zoe and Jamie. Then his parents—back home from their visit to his brother. They were all overjoyed that Connor had finally come to his senses and they were overflowing with love for the woman who had turned him back into their Connor again.

Zoe smiled to herself, remembering those precious nights

when Connor claimed he was overwhelmed by his house guests and needed the peace and quiet of the coach house. They would spend their wedding night here as well, before the family went home tomorrow and Zoe and Jamie formally moved into the big house with Connor.

Zoe could hear excited shouts coming from that same house and was glad she'd been firm about getting ready for her big day here—just her and Jamie with Jo to help them. This day was very special to her; her past had been long discarded now and she wanted to enjoy every single moment of the preparation. Over in the main house her bridesmaids—and, with Connor's brother and family over from Australia to join the rest, there were a *lot* of bridesmaids—were being showered, marshalled into their long pink dresses, having their hair brushed and threaded with flowers, but in the coach house all was serene.

One other thing had given Zoe so much more pleasure than she had expected. Connor had written to her mother and her new husband and they had been delighted to make the long journey up from the Channel Isles for the wedding. They had also asked Zoe, Connor and Jamie to come and stay with them for a holiday during the summer.

Jamie joined her at the window, peering out to see if it was time to go yet. He was happy all the time now. There were no more nightmares, no sheltering in a dark corner because he couldn't cope with the world. He was wearing his first grown-up, long-trousered suit today, with a flower in his buttonhole, just like Uncle Connor. And after the wedding— why, Uncle Connor would turn into Dad! Jamie couldn't wait!

Connor himself was a different man. The untrusting side of his character had passed. He loved his family; he saw so much more of his friends. The shadow that had darkened his life was now entirely gone. They might never have more children, but he had Zoe—and he knew her love was steadfast.

* * *

She could hear the church bells starting. 'Time to go,' said Jo, coming into the room behind her. 'The car's waiting outside and look—all your bridesmaids are parading beautifully across from the big house. I swear they think this wedding has been arranged just so they could have long dresses.'

Zoe chuckled. Arabella was leading them, taking her position as chief bridesmaid very seriously.

'Let's have a last look at you,' said Jo. A few tugs at the flow of the skirt, a slight adjustment of the veil and she nodded. 'I guess you'll do. Oh, Zoe, I'm so happy for you.'

Zoe saw tears in her friend's eyes and hugged her. 'I'm pretty happy myself,' she said. There weren't the words to express it any better. Her life was all happiness and sunlight.

Jo was to be Zoe's matron of honour. She had also been the chief organiser of this wedding. When Zoe had wondered if she and Connor should have 'just a quiet affair—nothing special', Jo had erupted.

'Rubbish! Connor loves you, he's proud of you; he wants the world to see you marry him. This wedding is going to be special!'

So now Zoe walked to the waiting Rolls-Royce, accompanied by Sam, who was to give her away. Jo guided the bridesmaids and their mothers into the next cars, and followed in the final one with Jamie.

The sound of the bells grew louder. Zoe wound down her window, waved at all the people who were waving at her. She had made so many friends in Buckley.

And then they were at the church gate.

There was just a moment standing in the churchyard while the bridesmaids were formed into lines by Jo and the photographer snapped pictures. Then the procession entered the church.

The organ notes swelled loud and proud. *Arrival of the Queen of Sheba.*

'I'm not the Queen of Sheba,' Zoe had protested.

'You are to me,' Connor had said.

Slowly, on Sam's arm, she walked down the red-carpeted aisle. She felt as if she would never stop smiling. And there ahead, stepping out to stand in front of the vicar, was Connor. By his side was the best man, his old friend Mick Baxter, who had flown from Patagonia. Well, that was what friends did.

Zoe reached Connor's side, lifted back her veil and smiled joyfully into his face. Connor's eyes were full of love as he took her hand in his. And she knew that all would be well. Now and for ever.

'Dearly beloved,' the vicar began…

0910/03a

# Medical Romance™

## BACHELOR OF THE BABY WARD
### by Meredith Webber

New to Jimmie's Children's Unit, anaesthetist Kate Armstrong is desperate not to fall for the sexy surgeon Angus McDowell – because she knows he'll be impossible to forget! But Angus' son has other ideas… All *he* wants is Kate to be his mummy…!

## FAIRYTALE ON THE CHILDREN'S WARD
### by Meredith Webber

Dear Santa, I've just learnt I have a daddy called Oliver, who works with my mummy Clare at Jimmie's Children's Unit. All I want is for my family to be together by Christmas Day! Love, Emily (aged 9¼)

## PLAYBOY UNDER THE MISTLETOE
### by Joanna Neil

Heartthrob Dr Ben Radcliffe is back in town and A&E doctor Jasmine knows she should stay well away, but it's impossible! As the snow starts to fall the village has their fingers crossed that the mistletoe at the village dance will work its Christmas magic!

## OFFICER, SURGEON…GENTLEMAN!
### by Janice Lynn

When Dr Amelia Stockton sees dashing naval surgeon and old flame Cole Stanley on board her ship, her heart calls mayday! Cole is aware of the Navy's 'no relationship' policy! But when it comes to the beautiful Amelia, rules are made to be broken!

**On sale from 1st October 2010**
**Don't miss out!**

*Available at WHSmith, Tesco, ASDA, Eason and all good bookshops*
*www.millsandboon.co.uk*

## MIDWIFE IN THE FAMILY WAY
### by Fiona McArthur

Emma has built a beautiful life for herself and her little girl in Lyrebird Lake. Gianni has come to the lake for a whistlestop tour, but is soon enchanted by the beautiful Emma. Will he be able to leave when he discovers she's expecting?

## THEIR MARRIAGE MIRACLE
### by Sue MacKay

Doctor Fiona is about to face Dr Tom Saville, her new boss – and the husband she hasn't seen for years. They were separated by heartbreak, but is Tom's incredible smile enough for Fiona to find the courage to take this second chance at happiness…?

## On sale from 1st October 2010
## Don't miss out!

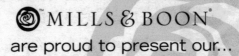

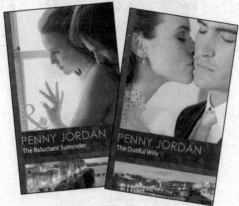

# Spend Christmas with NORA ROBERTS

Daniel MacGregor is the clan patriarch. He's powerful, rich – and determined to see his three career-minded granddaughters married. So he chooses three unsuspecting men he considers worthy and sets his plans in motion!

As Christmas approaches, will his independent granddaughters escape his schemes? Or can the magic of the season melt their hearts – and allow Daniel's plans to succeed?

## Available 1st October 2010

www.millsandboon.co.uk

# 2 FREE BOOKS
## AND A SURPRISE GIFT

We would like to take this opportunity to thank you for reading this Mills & Boon® book by offering you the chance to take TWO more specially selected books from the Medical™ series absolutely FREE! We're also making this offer to introduce you to the benefits of the Mills & Boon® Book Club™—

- **FREE home delivery**
- **FREE gifts and competitions**
- **FREE monthly Newsletter**
- **Exclusive Mills & Boon Book Club offers**
- **Books available before they're in the shops**

Accepting these FREE books and gift places you under no obligation to buy, you may cancel at any time, even after receiving your free books. Simply complete your details below and return the entire page to the address below. You don't even need a stamp!

**YES** Please send me 2 free Medical books and a surprise gift. I understand that unless you hear from me, I will receive 5 superb new stories every month including two 2-in-1 books priced at £4.99 each and a single book priced at £3.19, postage and packing free. I am under no obligation to purchase any books and may cancel my subscription at any time. The free books and gift will be mine to keep in any case.

Ms/Mrs/Miss/Mr _____ Initials _____

Surname _____

Address _____

_____

_____ Postcode _____

E-mail _____

Send this whole page to: Mills & Boon Book Club, Free Book Offer, FREEPOST NAT 10298, Richmond, TW9 1BR